KT-389-760

B
7

Scarlet Wilson wrote her first story aged eight and has never stopped. She's worked in the health service for twenty years, having trained as a nurse and a health visitor. Scarlet now works in public health and lives on the West Coast of Scotland with her fiancé and their two sons. Writing medical romances and contemporary romances is a dream come true for her.

RESISTING THE SINGLE DAD

SCARLET WILSON

MILLS & BOON

First published in Great Britain 2018
by Mills & Boon, an imprint of HarperCollins*Publishers*
1 London Bridge Street, London, SE1 9GF

Large Print edition 2018

© 2018 Scarlet Wilson

ISBN: 978-0-263-07307-2

MIX
Paper from
responsible sources
FSC
www.fsc.org   FSC® C007454

This book is produced from independently certified
FSC™ paper to ensure responsible forest management. For
more information visit www.harpercollins.co.uk/green.

Printed and bound in Great Britain
by CPI Group (UK) Ltd, Croydon, CR0 4YY

This book is dedicated to my editor,
Sheila Hodgson.

Thank you for looking after me so well in
the past year, and for being such a brilliant
advocate for the Medical Romance line.

Love you, Sheila!

CHAPTER ONE

CORDELIA GREENWAY RELAXED back into the chair as she tried to ignore the palpitations and light-headedness that had started. She breathed deeply and put her fingers to the side of her neck, massaging gently and closing her eyes as she waited for the manoeuvre to take effect.

Sweat started to run between her shoulder blades—another symptom. People were chatting all around her—no one seemed to have noticed her little 'turn'. And that was just the way she liked it. She hated fuss. She hated being under the spotlight.

So she stayed quiet, gently continuing to massage, and willing her heartbeat to steady. She probably should have glanced at her watch to time this—but she was so used to dealing with it, so used to keeping it under the radar, that it hadn't even entered her brain until now. She'd just gone into self-protect mode.

Her other hand lifted the hair off the back of her neck, where it was sticking. Ugh. But things were finally starting to work. She could almost hear out loud the beat of her heart starting to slow. Thank goodness.

After a few minutes she took a deep breath and rested her head on the cool desk for a second. Better. She tugged at her shirt, pulling it away from her body to let the air circulate. First thing she'd do when she got back home was jump in the shower.

There was a noise to her left. She stuck her head up above her cubby hole. Several of the other researchers were doing the same—they looked like a family of meerkats.

Professor Helier was pacing with his phone. The noise had come from his office. His voice squeaky. She didn't hesitate. She was at the glass door in seconds. 'Franc?'

Now he was nodding, scribbling things frantically on a piece of paper. He looked so pale. He swayed a little. She walked inside and held out her hands protectively behind him, in case he fell over. Professor Helier was the whole reason she was here.

When she'd found out that he was heading up the cardiac research at this lab, she *had* to be here. She would have done just about anything to work with this famed researcher.

But in the end all it had taken had been a few phone calls. She'd been head of the zebrafish research in the UK—leading the pioneering work into discovering their ability to regenerate heart muscle and how that could be transferred to humans. Professor Helier had embraced her interest instantly, inviting her to come and meet him, and asking if she wanted to lead one of his teams. She hadn't hesitated for a second.

The chance to work in Switzerland. The rich, clean air, snow-topped mountains, and a whole host of chocolates she should never touch. When she'd explained her reasons for working in cardiac research he'd just given her a beaming smile, and patted her hand. 'Cordelia, we all have our reasons for being here. That's what makes us all special.' He'd winked. 'That's what gives us all heart.' And the bad jokes had continued for the last three years.

He swayed a little again as he replaced the phone. She felt instantly protective. Franc must be approaching seventy and time hadn't been too kind to him. He always had a kind of frazzled appearance about him, along with his sometimes white coat and mass of grey hair. 'Franc, what is it? What can I do?'

No one knew exactly how old Franc Helier was. Even doing an internet search didn't help. He'd had the same mad grey hair and slim frame for the last forty years. Some of the junior staff joked that he looked like a mixture of Albert Einstein and a mad professor from a time travel movie. But for Cordelia it didn't matter. He was her friend. And she was his. That was all that mattered.

Franc put both hands on the desk. 'It's Emily,' he said a little breathlessly.

'Your sister?' He nodded, his expression a bit glazed. 'That was the hospital in Marseille. Apparently she collapsed at home and needs emergency surgery.'

Cordelia didn't hesitate. She lifted Franc's hat and coat from the hook behind her, thrusting them towards him. 'Go. Go now.' As he took them with slightly shaking hands she walked around his desk and opened his second drawer.

She really did know him like family. 'Here. Your passport. Do you want me to book you a flight and arrange a pick-up? I can book a hotel for you too.' She glanced at the name of the hospital written in scrawled script on the note. 'I'll find one near there.'

He blinked. And she reached out and touched his cheek. Franc had no other family. His wife had died ten years ago and all he had left was his sister. 'Go, Franc. Go be with your sister. Everything will be fine here. You know it will.'

He nodded nervously. 'Of course. I trust you, Cordelia. You know I do.'

She pulled up the collar of his jacket. 'I'll email you the details of the flight, transport and hotel. Just go home and pack a few things.'

He still looked a little stunned. Just what had they told him on the phone?

'Is there anything else I can do for you, Franc?'

It was almost as if she'd flicked a switch in his brain. 'The Japanese investors are coming on Tuesday. Drug trials AZ14 and CF10 need to be monitored, with all data recorded by midweek. There are clinics to cover.'

She smiled and touched his arm. 'I've got them. You know I've got them.'

His gaze met hers and it was the first time he'd looked a little more assured. Her illness had led her away from the traditional role of doctor. She'd spent years on wards dealing with her own symptoms, along with patients'. Long shifts and nights and nights of being on call had made her symptoms worse. When she'd finally realised she couldn't do the job she loved, she'd picked the next best thing. Her role here was fifty-fifty. Fifty per cent researcher and fifty per cent doctor in a well-supported, controlled environment. It suited her. It let her be involved in research that could make a difference for millions of patients around the world—herself included.

Franc gave a little jolt. He waved his hand at the chaos that was his desk. 'Oh, and we have a new doctor arriving. I'm supposed to pick them up at the airport.'

Cordelia winced and grabbed her notebook from her pocket. 'Is it Geneva?'

He nodded. She had to check. They had staff flying in from all around the world, and they didn't always arrive at the closest airport. 'What's the name?'

'Jeanne DuBois. It sounds French but it's American.' Something must have flashed into his brain. 'Oh.'

It was just the way he said it. 'What?' she questioned. 'What's "oh"?'

He pulled a face. 'They're supposed to stay with me. They were kind of a last-minute addition and hadn't managed to sort out accommodation yet.'

Cordelia swallowed, then nodded her head appropriately. She gave a smile. 'You're turning into an old cat lady, Franc. Taking in every waif and stray.'

She shook her head. Her own apartment's ceiling had collapsed last week after a neighbour upstairs had suffered a burst pipe. Franc had been gracious enough to let her stay in his own rambling mansion on the outskirts of Geneva. He often put up visiting researchers. Cordelia waved her hand. 'Leave it with me. That probably makes things easier anyway. It means when I pick them up, I get to drive back home. Oops.'

She put her hand up to her mouth as she realised what she'd said.

But Franc just shook his head and gave her shoulder a squeeze. 'My home is your home, Cordelia. It always will be. Here's hoping they take more than a month to fix your ceiling.' He closed his eyes for a second. 'It could be that soon you'll be the only family I have left.'

Her stomach flipped. This was serious. Part of her wished she'd heard that phone call. She reached over and gave Franc a bear hug. He felt so frail. So thin. Had he lost more weight and she hadn't noticed?

She whispered in his ear. 'I think of you as family too, Franc. Always remember that. You need something—I'm here.'

Franc nodded. 'Thank you, Cordelia.' He pulled himself free from her embrace and put on his hat and tucked his passport into his jacket. 'I'll call you.'

She shook her head. 'No, I'll message you. Go home and pack, and I'll arrange the flights and transfers. Head straight to the airport and I'll have things sorted by the time you get there.'

Franc nodded as he headed to the door. 'What

would I do without you?' He gave a shake of his head. 'Just glad I don't need to find out.'

Her heart gave a little twist as he headed to the elevators. She'd have to send out an email to let everyone know Franc had been called away for a few days. And she'd do that—just as soon as she'd organised the flights, hotel and transport. She spent the next twenty minutes online then messaged Franc.

A little pink sticky note was sitting in the debris on Franc's desk. She plucked it out and stared at it for a few seconds.

Geneva 20.00

She glanced at her watch. *Please tell me that isn't the flight for the visiting doctor.* She rummaged amongst the papers on the desk. Franc's desk had a notoriety all of its own. Some of the people who worked here thought that messages came to Franc's desk to die. It certainly seemed like that. It was extraordinary. In all his research studies he was fastidious. Meticulous. Cordelia always joked that Franc's desk was the one place he could leave his true mess behind.

Try as she might, she couldn't find any other notes that resembled airport pick-up times. Darn it. She grabbed her purse. She'd barely make it.

The last thing she wanted to do was leave this poor doctor stranded at the airport.

If she hurried, she might just get there in time…

The first flush of passengers exited through the gates to screams and yelps from people waiting. Cordelia always felt a little like a voyeur at these times—intruding on private family moments. The joy on some of the faces was beautiful. There were obviously a few more painful reunions. People embracing and bursting into sobs as they hugged each other. It made her heart ache.

She looked down at her hastily scrawled black letters. Jeanne Du Bois. She didn't even have any idea what age the doctor that was arriving from the US was. The only thing she was sure of was that they would be expecting Professor Helier, not a brunette in her thirties.

She people watched for a while. An elderly couple greeting adult children returning home.

A woman dropping her bags and running to-wards a guy, almost knocking him flat with her embrace. A few tourists, walking out with maps in hand and heading to the taxi rank.

And a guy, complete with cowboy boots and Stetson, wearing jeans and a dark grey T-shirt. He travelled wearing a *Stetson*?

She watched in amusement as he glanced around arrivals. He was tall. He really didn't need the Stetson to emphasise his height. As for those well-fitting jeans… She pulled her eyes away and focused on the door again, waiting to see if Jeanne Du Bois would appear. What would she look like? Probably tired. Most re-searchers who came from the US had to take two or three flights to get to Geneva.

She leaned against the barrier and tried not to dream of coffee and takeout food. She hadn't had time to eat before she'd left the research centre. Her stomach gave a growl just as the click of the cowboy boots came towards her.

A pair of deep brown eyes fixed on hers as he tipped his hat at her. He gestured towards the sign. 'I think you might be waiting for me.'

She blinked and looked down at her sign as if it might have changed while she wasn't looking.

He was close enough that she could smell his woody aftershave and see his sun-kissed skin. But it was the accent that threw her.

It was a thick American drawl. Like treacle. Or maple syrup. Something that smothered you in gorgeousness and just made you go…whoa.

She frowned as she tried not to let her herself be distracted by those very chocolaty eyes. Why was she associating everything with food? She was obviously hungrier than she'd thought.

'I'm waiting for a woman.' She looked down at her sign again, checking she hadn't been secretly pranked. Nope. It was still her writing. 'Jeanne Du Bois.'

The guy gave a lazy kind of smile and put his hand on his chest. 'I'm Jeanne Du Bois. Except it's G E N E. You know? Like Gene Kelly? Or Gene Hackman?'

She blinked. She still couldn't get over that accent. She wrinkled her nose. It reminded her of her favourite US TV series. 'Are you from Texas?'

He tipped his hat again. 'My mother was

French, but I'm a Texan through and through.' He held out his hand towards her. 'Pleased to meet you, ma'am. You've obviously dyed your hair, Professor Helier. And had a sex change,' he added with a wink.

Her brain sparked back into gear. 'Oh, yes. I'm sorry.' She shook his hand swiftly, the warm touch sending a little pulse up her arm. 'I'm Dr Cordelia Greenway, Professor Helier's second in command. I'm so sorry. He's had a family emergency, literally in the last few hours. I asked him who I was collecting at the airport and when he told me Jeanne Du Bois. I just assumed it was a woman.'

The guy shrugged. 'You're in Switzerland. I guess I can live with being mistaken for a woman.'

She wanted to laugh out loud. There was no chance of this guy being mistaken for a woman. Not when he looked, smelled and sounded like that.

She gestured around him. 'Where's your luggage? My car is in the car park just a few minutes from here. I can take you back to Professor Helier's house. I'm staying there too.'

For the briefest of seconds something flashed across his face. 'Oh.' He looked her up and down. 'Right. Yes…that's great.'

She felt heat rush into her cheeks. He was making assumptions. She shook her head frantically. 'Oh, no. No. Professor Helier and I are… friends. He's helping me out too. The ceiling in my apartment collapsed last week.'

Gene's eyebrows rose. 'Oh, no. What a nightmare.'

She nodded and smiled. 'Yip. And my upstairs neighbour is off on a round-the-world cruise for a month. And still doesn't know about her leaking pipe, or the fact the factor had to break down her door to get in and switch her water off.'

Gene glanced over his shoulder, then looked back at her. 'So where does that leave you?'

'Homeless. Wet. With water pouring down my walls and ruining my carpets and electrics.' She raised her hand and shook her head. 'No, really, the water might have been turned off, but until my neighbour is back and our insurance companies can battle it out together…' She let her words trail off.

He nodded. 'You're kind of stuck?' He took off his cowboy hat to reveal short brown hair that he ran his hand through. 'I guess that means that Professor Helier doesn't really have a lot of room.'

She held up her hands. 'It's fine. Really it is. Honestly, his house isn't a house—it's a kind of rambling mansion. It's the kind of place they read you fairy stories about when you're a kid. He has plenty of space.' She wiggled her hand. 'Not all of it habitable. But there are rooms next to mine that are comfortable. You'll be fine.' She looked back at the doors. 'Do you want to collect your luggage and we'll go?'

He gave her a nod and stuck his hat back on his head. 'Are you okay to help me with the cases?'

She was a little surprised. 'Just how many did you bring?'

He smiled. 'Just one each.'

She blinked and looked behind him. 'One each? There's someone else with you?'

A wave of concern swept his face. 'You mean Professor Helier didn't tell you?'

She felt her stomach flip over. She was so

looking forward to getting home, eating something takeout and climbing into her pyjamas.
She didn't need any more unexpected turns
right now. Not when she needed to be up at six
a.m. to prepare for the patients attending clinic
tomorrow. She almost didn't want to say the
words out loud. 'Tell me what?'

'That I wasn't coming alone?' He sounded
nervous.

She half expected some beauty queen to
emerge from the arrivals hall with a stunning
full-length gown, silver heels and blonde hair
tumbling down her back. After all, he looked
like a guy who would inevitably be dating some
kind of beauty queen.

She swallowed. Wine. Maybe she'd have some
wine instead of coffee when she got back.

'No.' She tried to sound friendly. 'He didn't
mention it.' She looked around him again. 'Is
your wife just freshening up?'

He gave her a quizzical glance. 'Oh, he really didn't tell you. It's not my wife. I don't
have a wife. It's my son, Rory. He's sleeping.
One of the airline staff is minding him while I

checked to see if our pick-up was here. I guess that's you.'

'Your son?'

She couldn't help it. She hadn't meant it to sound like that. Of course some of the visiting doctors brought their partners or families when they came to stay. It just wasn't like Professor Helier to miss such an important detail. It just let her know how distracted he'd actually been.

Gene gave her a little frown. 'Is that going to be a problem? I'm happy to call a cab and check into a local hotel. I don't want to put you to any trouble.'

It was the tone of his voice. He was annoyed. And no wonder. He'd been travelling for hours to a strange city, a new job—and she wasn't exactly being welcoming.

She held up her hand. 'It's no problem. If you want to get your son, I can manage the cases.'

For a few seconds he just stared at her, almost as if he was trying to decide whether to believe her or not. But she could see the fatigue on his face. She had a cheek to feel tired when he'd just crossed the Atlantic to get here. No wonder his son was sleeping. Gene Du Bois probably wanted to be sleeping too.

He gave a nod and headed back to the doors. A perfectly groomed stewardess met him with the child in her arms. Gene took the sleeping little figure easily, letting him snuggle into his shoulder, with one arm under his legs. He grabbed a large navy blue case with one hand as the stewardess brought out another—bright green with a lion on front.

Cordelia smiled as she felt a little pang. Kids. She normally managed to circumvent them. Having an ongoing cardiac condition wasn't exactly conducive to having kids, and the older she got, the more she thought about it.

She'd learned to distance herself. It was easier that way. There was less chance of seeing what she'd miss out on. Less chance of becoming bitter about what could never be hers.

But she couldn't exactly circumvent a kid in the same house as her.

She hurried over and grabbed the bright green suitcase, trundling it behind her, and tried to keep up with Gene Du Bois's long strides.

'Dr Du Bois, Professor Helier didn't let me

know what programme you'll be contributing to. I'll need to make some introductions and ensure everything has been put in place for you. Can you let me know what research you're involved in?'

Gene gave her a sideways glance and slowed his steps. 'I'm beginning to wonder if this was a good idea. I came here because the Reuben Institute is supposed to be at the forefront of cardiac research. I'm here for a month, to take the lead on the cardiomyopathy studies.'

She couldn't help but pull a face. 'Listen, I know this might seem chaotic, but the only thing that's normally chaotic at the Reuben Institute is Professor Helier's desk. Everything else is ruthlessly efficient, I assure you.'

They crossed the road towards the car park. 'What project do you lead on?'

She winced as her stomach grumbled loudly. 'The zebrafish studies.' She opened the car door. 'How about we put aside cardiac studies for this evening? I have to confess to not being much of a cook. Would the little guy eat pizza if I picked some up for us on the way back to the house?'

Gene settled the little boy into the car and strapped him in, with barely a murmur from his son. He ruffled his son's hair. 'Rory happens to be a big fan of pizza. After nearly twenty hours' travelling, I'm willing to do takeout.'

Cordelia gave a thankful nod and climbed into the car. 'Great. We should be home in twenty minutes. Settle in. The scenery is outstanding.'

She paused for a second and couldn't help but ask the question that had been swimming around her head since she'd first seen him. 'So, Dr Du Bois, do you always do full cowboy when you travel?'

He took off his hat as he climbed into the car and gave her a wink. 'What can I say? I'm from Texas.'

Gene wasn't quite sure what to think. He was beginning to regret dragging his little guy halfway across the planet to be involved in this research project. Professor Helier had guaranteed everything would be in place—including a suitable day-care arrangement for Rory.

Gene leaned back in the comfortable seat and closed his eyes for a few seconds. Maybe he should be watching the gorgeous scenery, but twenty hours of jet-lag was rapidly catching up with him. It had already made him more than a little short with his hostess. His momma would be spinning in her grave and slapping the back of his head right now.

No one could believe when his French scientist mother had fallen for a Texas cowboy—least of all her. Moving from Paris to Houston, Texas had been a culture shock for her. And after ten years and still no wedding ring, she'd finally bailed.

So Gene had spent his life between two continents. And he'd considered himself lucky. Flitting between a ranch in Texas and the city of Paris hadn't exactly been hard. As a child he'd excelled in living on two continents. And even though his father had been disappointed his son wanted to study medicine instead of ranching, he knew his dad had still been secretly proud.

The only thing that had really swept the feet from under him had been the message three years ago from the fellow doctor he'd had a fling with at a cardiac conference. Mindy had suffered from congenital hypertrophic cardiomyopathy. Pregnancy should never have been on her life plan. But when she'd found herself pregnant with Rory after a few passionate nights together in Istanbul, she'd chosen to go ahead with the pregnancy.

She'd only contacted Gene when things had got desperate. Everyone had advised her not to go ahead, knowing exactly what the strain of a pregnancy would do to her. Sure enough, soon after Rory had been born, she'd ended up on the heart transplant list.

And when she'd gone into complete heart failure, she'd finally contacted Gene to let him know about his son.

He'd been angry. He'd been furious. But how furious could a guy be at someone who was clearly dying?

His life had turned upside down in an instant. One look at the nine-month-old cheeky little blond baby, pulling himself up on wobbly legs to the side of his mother's bed, had been all the time he'd needed to make a decision.

It didn't help that in the interim since the conference he'd actually met someone. Karen. An anaesthetist at Boston General where he was working. They'd moved in together. Had had tentative talks about the future. He'd even considered buying a ring.

But the unexpected son had been a bolt out of the blue that Karen could never have expected. She'd been shocked—and then walked away. And he couldn't blame her. They'd discussed the fact they might like a family in the future—but Karen wasn't ready to deal with one that had been thrust on her. So after a year of being in a settled relationship he'd found himself alone.

Mindy had died three weeks later. And Gene had immediately set about turning his life around.

A single dad working in a hospital environment wasn't exactly conducive to good parenting.

He'd never considered working in research up until that point. But knowing that his son carried the gene for cardiomyopathy was enough to put his priorities in order. He'd spent the last three years with his dad joking about Gene looking at genes.

But that was fine, because he'd spend the rest

of his life looking at genes if it could help his son and any future grandkids.

He smiled to himself. Rory had just turned four. Four. And he was thinking about grand-kids. But he was a doctor, he had to plan ahead. And every plan in his life now included Rory.

He opened his eyes and glanced at the woman driving the car. Cordelia Greenway. He was sure he'd seen her name on some of the research pa-pers published by the Reuben Institute. She'd said she was Professor Helier's second in com-mand.

Gene had learned to take things in his stride. He'd had to. Life frequently threw curve balls. He didn't mind curve balls. What he did mind was feeling as if his son was an unwanted extra. Maybe he was just being too sensitive? Or maybe he was being overprotective. But he was sure there had been a look of…something flash across Cordelia's face when he'd men-tioned his son.

It could just be that she'd been taken un-awares. But his gut told him something else. His gut could almost sense her take about ten steps back. And he didn't like that. He didn't like that at all.

He wasn't crazy. He didn't expect the whole world to love his son the way he did. Some folks just didn't do kids. He got that. But he would never tolerate anyone making his four-year-old feel unwelcome. Long journey or not, if he had to, he'd jump on the next flight back to Texas. Getting a job was never a problem. Getting the *right* job was more important than anything.

He gave himself a shake as she pulled the car up outside a pizza parlour. She turned around and gave him a nervous kind of smile. 'What's your poison?' she asked. 'This place is great. Everything's fresh and their pizzas are to die for.'

He drew in a deep breath. She was making an effort, and it was clear he made her a bit nervous. He dug into his pocket for his wallet, but she shook her head and waved her hand. 'Don't be silly. You just got here. This is on me.' She bit her bottom lip and nodded towards the sleeping figure in the back seat. 'What about Rory?'

Gene glanced at his son again and felt his heart swell. This little guy was his life. One look of that cheeky little face could brighten the darkest day.

'Just cheese and ham for him. I'll have whatever the Swiss equivalent of a meat feast is.'

Cordelia gave him a nod and ducked out of the car. 'No problem. Give me five minutes.'

She walked into the pizza parlour and he leaned back in the seat again, watching as she interacted with the servers. She seemed at home here—it was obvious that they knew her. She leaned on the counter, giving him a prime view of her curves visible in her pink fitted shirt and black trousers. He gave a small smile. She'd probably look great in a pair of jeans.

Her fingers toyed with a strand of chestnut-brown hair as she chatted. For the first time he looked at her left hand. No ring. Nothing. She'd said they would all be staying in Professor Helier's mansion. Did she have a partner already there? Or would she be there alone with him and Rory?

His stomach gave a little clench. Maybe that was part of her discomfort. She'd clearly expected a woman to arrive at Geneva airport.

Maybe being alone with a strange guy and kid had completely thrown her.

After another five minutes she slid back into the car with the pizza boxes. 'Do you mind holding these until we reach the house? It will only be another five minutes.'

He nodded and started to pay attention to the scenery as they drove through the outskirts of Geneva. The buildings and architecture were stunning, a mixture of Gothic spires and brand-new glass towers. All this with a backdrop of snow-topped mountains against a darkening sky.

The road gradually became a little more rural and Cordelia indicated and turned through a pair of elaborate iron gates and continued on down a long driveway. Thick green trees lined the driveway, with extensive grounds all around them. After a few minutes a dark house seemed to emerge out of nowhere.

Gene couldn't help but smile. It was like a real Gothic-style mansion—straight out of a Dracula-style movie. Gargoyles adorned some of the dark grey stonework around the myriad thin windows lining the front of the house. A huge, imposing double door, painted black with a large knocker, was right in front of them.

Cordelia pulled up directly outside and turned to face him. It was the first time she'd looked a little more relaxed since they'd met.

She held out her hand towards the house. 'Here it is. And I'll say it before you do. Dracula's mansion. The inside is much more welcoming than the outside. You'll love it.' She glanced nervously over her shoulder towards Rory again. 'And I'm sure he will too.' She shot him a big smile. It only seemed a little forced. 'Welcome to Switzerland, Dr Du Bois.'

CHAPTER TWO

SHE WAS BABBLING AGAIN. It was ridiculous. She was a thirty-one-year-old experienced doctor. She had absolutely no reason to be nervous. But somehow the cowboy from Texas with the blond kid had totally knocked her sideways.

She unlocked the front door and switched off the alarm. Rory was tucked up on his dad's shoulder again. 'Do you want to put him straight to bed?' she asked, praying that the beds in the guest quarters were made up.

Gene shook his head. 'No. I want to wake him up and feed him before letting him sleep right through. I always find it's best to try and acclimatise as soon as possible.'

She blinked. 'You move about a lot?'

He shrugged as he glanced around the wide entranceway and huge staircase leading to the upper floors. 'I have done. Rory will be going to school next year, so I'll need to have a rethink.

But so far he's been in nursery in the US, the UK and France. He seems to have loved them all.'

She gave a careful nod of her head. 'Wow. That's a lot.' She hesitated then pointed towards the rooms to the right. 'The formal kind of sitting rooms are that way. But how about we grab the pizzas and go through to the kitchen? The bedrooms are all upstairs, I'll show you them soon.'

Gene glanced back out to the car. She waved her hand. 'I can grab the cases.'

'No way.' His Texas drawl almost stopped her in her tracks. 'There's no way I'm letting you get them. Let me sit Rory down at the table. He's waking up anyway. Can you get him a drink of water while I grab the cases?'

She nodded quickly and showed him through to the extensive black and white kitchen, with old-fashioned wooden table in the middle, pulling out the high-backed chairs for him to settle Rory.

The little boy watched her with suspicious eyes as she opened the cupboard and nearly pulled out a glass, before changing her mind at the last moment and swapping the glass for a mug. She grabbed a bottle of water from the fridge then filled the mug and sat down next to him. She couldn't help but feel nervous. What did you talk to a four-year-old about? And the truth was she was a little curious about this little kid. Would he have an accent like his father? 'Hi, Rory, I'm Cordelia. I'm going to be working with your daddy.'

She flipped open the lid of the smallest pizza box. 'We got you ham and cheese pizza. Your dad said you'd like that. Would you like some?' She pulled a slice of the pizza free and left it for him to grab himself.

Rory watched her with dark eyes for a few moments. It was unnerving what the gaze of a four-year-old could do to her. She didn't blame him. He'd literally just woken up, and was in completely strange surroundings. And she'd seen those big brown eyes before. Rory definitely had his father's eyes.

She could hear Gene rolling the suitcases inside then closing the main door behind him. He strode through to the kitchen and sat down next to Rory, ruffling his hair again as he looked at the pizza boxes. 'Which one is mine? Come on. Eat up, little guy. You must be starving.'

Rory stared at him. 'Where's the French fries?'

Cordelia almost laughed out loud—there was a definite hint of a Texan accent, but there was also a little bit more. Gene said they'd stayed in France and the UK too. It seemed the little boy had picked up a little of everything. She stood up and flicked the switch on the kettle and glanced over at Gene. 'Do you want a cup of tea or coffee?'

Gene shook his head. 'I'll stick to water, thanks. I want to try and sleep a little tonight.'

Rory stopped staring at her suspiciously now his dad was back and picked up a slice of pizza. He leaned his head on one hand. 'Where's my bed?'

Gene glanced at her and Cordelia answered quickly. 'It's upstairs. There are two rooms, so you can either go in a room on your own or you can go in with your dad.'

Her stomach gave a little flip. She still didn't know if the rooms were ready or not. Franc had a housekeeper who kept the place tidy. If he'd told her in advance she would have the rooms ready.

'Give me five minutes,' she said, bolting down a bite of pizza and running up the stairs.

She flicked on all the lights as she ran down the corridor, past her own rooms and on to the other guest bedrooms. The door were already open—always a good sign. She checked the first. The bed had been made up in pale blue, with a pile of white towels, some soap and a toothbrush and toothpaste in the bathroom next door.

The second room had been made up in pale green. There was a teddy sitting on the bed next to the pillow. It was slightly threadbare, but it was something. She sighed in relief. At some point Franc must have remembered—even if he hadn't this afternoon. At least the rooms were ready. She could sort out everything else to-morrow.

By the time she got back down the stairs, Rory was back in his father's arms, a half-eaten slice of pizza on the table.

'Is he out for the count again?'

Gene nodded. 'Everything okay upstairs?' he asked warily.

She nodded. 'Yes, just checking the rooms. Everything is perfect. I was just worried in case Franc hadn't mentioned to the housekeeper about your arrival. But he must have remembered. The rooms are fine.'

Gene followed her up the stairs and laid Rory down on the green bed. He sat for a few seconds, stroking his blond hair and just watching him.

It felt like she was intruding. Watching a moment that should be shared just between a parent and child.

He turned to face her. 'What time are we going to the institute tomorrow? I need to know so I can get us up and ready in time.'

Her brain automatically revised her usual plans. If she told them she was usually there from six a.m. until seven at night they would think she was crazy. Or sad. Or both. 'I normally go in around eight a.m. I like to be available to check on any of the patients involved in the trials before they get started for the day.

Would you be okay if we had breakfast just after seven?'

He nodded. 'That's fine. We'll probably be up early anyway. Your morning will be our afternoon.'

She felt a wave of panic. 'Rory—what does he eat for breakfast?'

Gene shrugged. 'Whatever you've got. Cereal, toast, eggs. He's happy with just about anything.'

'If you write a list tomorrow, the housekeeper will get you whatever you need for him. I'm not sure just how many child-friendly foods we'll have in the house right now.'

Gene looked over at her in the dim light. She could see the shadows under his eyes. He must be just as tired as Rory was.

A million questions were burning in her brain. Where was Rory's mother? Why hadn't he mentioned her at all?

There was a hint of bristle along his jawline. She watched as he leaned over Rory and kissed him gently on the head, the muscles on his chest and arms visible beneath the thin soft cotton T-shirt.

Her skin prickled. It wasn't like her to notice things like that. Of course she wasn't blind. Of course she'd had a few relationships in the past. But she'd never been the kind of girl to really notice a guy. To look at his eyes. To look at his build. To notice the way he looked at his son.

She gave herself a shake. She was being ridiculous.

It looked like Gene could be a while, so she backed out of the door into the corridor.

She had work to do. Plenty to distract her in the meantime. Cardiac research could easily stop her thinking about the man with the accent as thick as syrup and his equally cute young son.

She gave herself a shake and hurried back to the kitchen, pulling a stack of paperwork from her bag.

Work. That's where she was always safest. She should concentrate on that.

Rory had snored peacefully all night while Gene had slept fitfully. It always took him a few days to be comfortable enough in his surroundings to sleep well. It didn't help that his mind had kept drifting to the chestnut-haired woman with the bright green eyes.

He still wasn't sure about her. If Professor Helier wasn't going to be around he'd give her a day, then decide if he was staying or not. He'd learned not to waste time in this life.

Rory got ready eagerly, jumping into a pair of bright green shorts and his favourite baseball shirt and hat while Gene showered. He generally liked to dress a little more informally at work, but first impressions always lasted, so he left his Stetson on the dresser and pulled on work clothes more fitting for a cardiac physician.

By the time they reached the kitchen, Cordelia was already there, humming to herself as the coffee percolated and she popped some bread in the toaster. The kitchen table was set with cutlery, some cereals, a jug of milk and some butter, jam and marmalade. She even had a little pad and pen with 'Shopping list' written across the top.

She smiled as they appeared. 'Good morning. Hi, Rory, did you sleep well last night?'

Rory started. It was almost as if he'd forgotten that he'd met her last night. Gene pulled out a chair for him. Cordelia had the sides of her hair pulled back in a clip and she was wearing a red dress and black suit jacket. The dress ended just on her knees and he blinked in surprise at her red baseball boots.

She laughed at his expression. 'I know. I know. I had a problem with my feet a few years ago. I find baseball boots comfiest.' She pointed to a pair of medium-heeled black shoes at the side of the kitchen, 'But I promise I'll change before we leave.'

'What happened to your feet?' Rory asked immediately, while Gene cringed.

There was the briefest uncomfortable blink from Cordelia then she gave a small shrug. 'A very long time ago I was a ballet dancer. And when you're a ballet dancer you go right up on your tippy-toes.' She opened one palm and put the tips of the fingers of her other hand in the centre. 'But when you do that when you're still young it does damage to your toes.' She pulled a face. 'So my feet are quite ugly. But...' she waved down at her shoes '...it gives me a chance to wear my favourite baseball boots.'

Gene felt a bit warmer. She seemed a little

more relaxed this morning. More amenable. Maybe she'd got her head around sharing this house with a stranger and his kid.

Rory stared at her. 'I like them,' he said as he shot a glance at his dad. Gene almost laughed out loud. He knew exactly what was coming.

'I wanted red baseball boots, but my dad wouldn't get me any.'

Cordelia grabbed the toast as it popped and put it on a plate, carrying it over to the table with the coffee pot. She raised her eyebrows and gave Rory a conspiratorial glance. 'He wouldn't? Why ever not?'

She sounded easy. She sounded comfortable around them, but Gene noticed a tiny twitch at the side of her eye. She might be acting as if everything was fine, but she was still a little nervous. Why?

He picked up a piece of toast for Rory and started buttering it for him, smiling at his son the whole time. 'I didn't buy him a pair of red baseball boots because we already have a pair of blue and a pair of green.'

'You have?' Cordelia ducked her head under the table.

She frowned as she sat up. 'But those aren't baseball boots.'

Rory smiled as he picked up his toast. 'Yeah. I put on my runners today. I decided I might need to be real quick.'

Gene poured some of the coffee into the mugs on the table. 'Why would you need to be quick, Rory?'

Rory bit his toast and chewed for a few seconds before he answered in a whisper. 'Because there might be…girls.'

Cordelia choked at the other side of the table, putting her hand over her mouth, her cheeks getting pinker and pinker. Gene watched in amusement. 'Okay?'

She nodded and jumped up, grabbing a glass for some water. 'Yes. Sorry.' She smiled as she looked back at Rory. 'I just wasn't expecting that one.'

Gene leaned forward on the table, looking between his son and Cordelia. He ruffled Rory's hair again. 'Dad,' said Rory, trying to shake him off, 'stop that.'

Gene pulled his hand back and shrugged at Cordelia. 'Apparently, it doesn't matter what nursery or day care Rory goes to—his blond hair makes all the girls say he is cute.'

'I'm not cute. I'm four,' said Rory quickly.

Cordelia grinned as she sat down again. 'I think four is kind of cute.'

Rory rolled his eyes. 'Oh, not you too.'

Gene pulled a face at her and bent down to whisper in Rory's ear. 'Watch out, Rory. She might be like those other girls. She might want to kiss you.'

Rory gave a shudder and Cordelia laughed out loud. It was almost as if he could see the knot in her shoulders start to loosen.

They finished breakfast quickly and Gene scribbled a list for the housekeeper. 'Remember red apples, Dad. And 'nanas.' Gene added bananas to the list as Rory stuck his arms into his jacket. He was proud at how articulate his little boy was, but there were still some words that seemed like tongue-twisters to a four-year-old.

He swung Rory up into his arms. 'Ready?'

Rory held up his fist and Gene bumped his against it. It was their move. Their superhero move.

Cordelia's brow was wrinkled as she watched

them. She had kind of a bewildered smile on her face as she stood next to the alarm, ready to punch in the code. 'Let's go then, guys.'

For the last week she'd breakfasted with Franc. It had been a much more genteel and sedate experience. This morning had been entirely different.

And it made her feel…odd.

She was getting to the stage in life where most of her friends had kids. Those who knew her best had enough awareness to realise that she occasionally found things tough. It wasn't that she completely avoided kids. Of course she couldn't. She just didn't generally have them under her nose.

So this was different.

And even though part of her stomach twisted and turned, it was also nice. And that was unexpected.

This morning's breakfast had been noisy, chaotic and maybe even a little fun.

They travelled the distance to the institute easily. It was close enough to the city centre for public transport but far enough away to be spacious and have adequate parking.

The institute employed more than three hundred staff. Physicians, nurses, researchers and admin staff. There was also a small day-care centre, which she prayed that Franc had remembered to book Rory into.

Helene, the woman in charge, gave the briefest of pauses when they entered, before putting a beaming smile on her face. 'Ah, yes. Professor Helier mentioned that we might be getting a new recruit.' She gave Gene a questioning smile. 'I think he said for a month?'

Gene nodded. 'Yes, my contract is just for a month.'

It was odd. Cordelia could tell he was a little nervous—but Rory clearly wasn't. He might say he didn't want to play with girls, but he wandered off straight away to go and join a group of kids. Helene walked quickly over to a desk and pulled out some paperwork and a pager. Gene smiled as he took it. 'Haven't had one of these since I was a hospital physician.'

Helene gave him a nod. 'It's just for the first few days. It means I can get hold of you quickly if Rory doesn't settle.' She ran through the paperwork, requesting medical history, allergies, immunisations and any special requirements. Rory was already babbling away in French to his counterparts. The kids in Switzerland spoke a whole variety of languages. It was fortunate that Rory had already spent some time in France.

Cordelia put her hand on Gene's shoulder. 'You okay?'

His eyes were fixed on Rory. He gave a nervous laugh as his dark brown eyes met hers. 'Sure I am. The little guy never seems to have any problems fitting in. I just worry.'

Cordelia was curious. 'Rory never stays with his mum?'

The look he gave her made her want to pull back the inquisitive words. What was it with her and this guy? He bit his bottom lip and put his head down, completing the paperwork, checking his pager was working and finishing with Helene.

Her skin prickled at the awkwardness of it all. He was new. They had visiting fellows at the Rueben Institute all the time. The institute was renowned. Their last Professor had won a special prize for his research. They had many joint projects with university hospitals across the globe. People wanted to work here. She counted herself lucky that she'd managed to secure a permanent position. If Gene Du Bois was going to be here for a month he'd have to lose a little of his prickliness.

She walked him out across the granite-floored, glass-fronted foyer. Above them was a glass atrium, showing the four floors of the institute.

She ignored the earlier hiccup and held out her hands. 'Okay, Dr Du Bois, welcome to the Rueben Institute. Now that Rory is settled, let me show you around.'

Darn it. For some reason his tongue had stuck to the roof of his mouth and he'd been unable to answer her question. Last time he'd been tongue-tied he'd been around fourteen. This was ridiculous.

But what was even more ridiculous was the thought that had shot into his head when she'd asked about Rory's mother.

He literally had the story off pat. He'd been asked on numerous occasions where Rory's mom was. It was a sad story. But lots of kids all over the world had only one parent. It wasn't the biggest deal in the world.

But this time, when he'd been asked, he'd just frozen. Maybe it was those green eyes. Maybe it was the shiny brown hair and the way it looked so good with her red dress. Maybe it was those darned curves in that red dress that seemed to make a swishy kind of noise every time she took a step—daring him to look at the swing of her hips.

Or maybe it was the tiny freckles running across the bridge of her nose.

Whatever it was, it was something.

He was tired. That was all. Probably jet-lagged too. Maybe it wasn't a good idea to start straight away. Perhaps he should have given them a few days to settle in. But, then again, Rory looked like he'd settled already. And Gene couldn't help but be proud of the way his son had naturally babbled away in French to the other kids.

He pulled his eyes away from the swinging hips in front of him and looked up at the impressive foyer. He'd seen pictures of the institute before. But he hadn't really expected this.

Cordelia had walked over to the back of the institute—or what should be the back wall of the institute. Instead of brick, there was a wall entirely of glass, letting the bright morning light stream in and giving a picture-perfect view of the Alps in the distance. It was like capturing a holiday snap. Or picking up a picture postcard.

The view was breathtaking. And unexpected. She gave him a nod as she stood alongside him. She sucked in a deep breath. 'Whenever I get exasperated at work, or fed up, I always like to remember how lucky I am to work here.'

He stood for a few minutes, his eyes scanning the horizon. It was like taking a chill pill. He'd been on edge, agitated about the arrangements and worried about how they might affect Rory. But standing here, watching this, it was almost as if someone had just put his head on a lavender pillow and told him to relax and calm down.

He'd wanted to come here. He'd wanted to work with Professor Helier. And even if Professor Helier wasn't here, the rest of his team was.

He glanced sideways at Cordelia. She was

smiling, drinking in the scenery that she obviously saw every day. 'It never gets old,' she said quietly. 'Every day is a new day, with a world of possibilities.'

He pressed his lips together and asked the question that was burning in his mind. 'You said you're Professor Helier's second in command. What's your background?'

She turned to face him with an amused expression. 'What is this? An interview?'

She gestured towards the glass staircase leading up to the next floor.

'Maybe.' He shrugged.

She nodded her head thoughtfully. 'Okay, then. But it works both ways. Deal?'

He held his hand out towards her. 'Deal.' The warmth from her fingers almost made him shudder, especially as they brushed against the inside of his wrist.

Cordelia walked up the stairs ahead of him. He had to tell himself not to focus on her legs. Or her hips. Or her...

She started talking and broke into his wayward thoughts. 'I'm a physician. I trained in the UK.'

'I take it your speciality was cardiology.'

She nodded. 'Of course. And yours?'

He gave the briefest of smiles. 'The same.'

She hesitated for a second. 'I always had a special interest in cardiology.' She gave a nonchalant wave of her hand. 'Family stuff. So I decided to get into research.' She hesitated once again and he was instantly curious as her eyes went up to the left for a second. Wasn't that supposed to be a sign of thinking or processing?

They reached the top of the stairs and she took them down a different wing of the building. 'This is the research labs.' She gave a little smile. 'This is where I get lost in the wonder of zebrafish and what incredible creatures they are.' She gave a little sigh. 'If only us humans had the power of healing and regeneration like they do.'

He stopped at the front doors of the lab and looked inside. As expected, it was white and pristine. There were several rooms. Laboratories where clinical scientists were processing blood tests. A vast room filled with computers where information was obviously being processed and analysed. In the middle of the room was an unusual spiral-shaped fish tank. Even from here he could see the tiny zebrafish swimming around.

He tilted his head to the side and looked at Cordelia curiously. It was almost as if she expected the question. 'They teach us so much. And they give us hope. Professor Helier thought it was important that people didn't just watch them in a lab. He wanted us all to appreciate them. That's why he commissioned the special tank for right in the middle of the room.'

Gene nodded thoughtfully. 'So many people are against research involving animals.'

'And so many people would be right. Here, we don't harm the zebrafish in any way. But we watch them. We learn from them and their DNA. And we try to replicate what they can do in a lab environment.'

He leaned against the wall and folded his arms. 'I like the ethics here. I knew that before I came. It was one of the things that made me want to be part of the team—even if it is just for a short spell.'

Her phone pinged and she pulled it from her pocket, frowning.

'What's wrong?' Her skin had paled and when she looked up her eyes were kind of watery.

She pressed her lips together. He could tell she was trying to keep it together. 'Professor Helier's sister has terminal cancer. She's his only living family. He's going to stay with her. He's going to look after her.'

Gene felt his heart clench. It was selfish—he knew it. But part of the reason he'd come here had been to work with this man—to learn from him.

'What does that mean?'

She blinked back the obvious tears as she tucked her phone back into her pocket. 'It means that I'll have to email everyone in the institute. Franc—he wants to call you tonight.' Her bright green eyes met his. There was something in them. A wariness, but also a tiny hint of desperation. 'The monitoring of the cardiomyopathy patients is at a really crucial stage. I suspect he's going to ask if you'll take over as head of the trial.' Her voice was a little shaky.

He reached over and touched her arm. 'Cordelia? Are you okay?'

She nodded and brushed the side of her eye.

'Of course I am. I'm just being silly. I'm worried about Franc and how he'll cope with nursing his sister.' She held out her hands. 'This place is virtually his life.' She gave her head a shake. 'I just don't want to let him down in his absence. The work here is so important to so many people.'

It was the way she said the words. Everyone who worked here would be passionate about what they did. But there seemed to be a real emphasis on her words. As if there was something that he was missing.

And he got it. He got it better than anyone. Because the work on cardiomyopathy could end up being a lifeline for his son.

He watched her carefully. He could almost see her shaking off the overspill of emotions, tidying them back up and putting them in a box. His stomach roiled a little. It was the weirdest thing, but it was almost the same expression she'd had on her face at one point last night. He just couldn't understand why.

And he definitely couldn't understand why he was so curious.

She licked her lips and looked at him again.

'My turn to ask the questions. I'm sure that Franc knew all this back to front. But I don't. What's your background?'

For a second he felt himself move into self-protect mode. The bit where he only gave the edited version of his life.

But he turned around as she led him back from the research wing and he was faced with the picture-postcard landscape again. The world was so vast out there. He was only a tiny bit of it. Why on earth did he feel he had something to hide?

He stopped walking and his fingers brushed against her elbow. She turned to face him. He almost laughed.

Yip. He was currently in a movie of his life. Cordelia was the heroine in this movie and she was standing in front of a green screen. Because this background was just too perfect to be real.

And as he stood a little longer, she began to look too perfect too. She was sharply in focus. Now he could appreciate the long, dark lashes. Now he could appreciate the smudge of red lipstick still on her lips.

Now…he was definitely losing his mind.

It was almost like hovering above and watching, instead of really taking part.

He shook his head. 'I trained as a physician in Texas but lived my life between France and Texas. My mom—*ma mère*—was a French scientist. Somehow she managed to meet my rancher father and I lived between two continents.'

She tilted her head to the side. 'Wow. That's some childhood.'

He nodded. 'I was lucky. I had barrel loads of love on both sides of the Atlantic. I had friends in Houston and in Paris.'

'So what made you become a doctor?'

They walked along the corridor towards the other wing. 'Oh, I always wanted to be a doctor. Right from when I was a little kid. My dad wanted me to take over the ranch and while I love it, my heart was never in it. Thankfully I've got a stepbrother who has ranch blood running in his veins.'

'Oh, okay.' He could see the obvious question running around in her head. He could avoid it— or ignore it—like he had before. But he had a reason for being here. He was invested in this research. And there was almost an ethical responsibility to say why.

He stopped walking. 'Rory's mom was a fellow doctor I met at a conference. We had a few nights together and then didn't keep in touch. I met Rory when he was nine months old. Mindy had hypertrophic cardiomyopathy. She was already in a degree of heart failure when she became pregnant and was advised not to continue with the pregnancy. I had no idea she was unwell and she didn't listen. And she only contacted me when she'd been on the heart transplant list for a few months.'

Cordelia's eyes were wide. He just kept going. It was easier to have it out there. 'Three weeks later Mindy died. And it's been just me and Rory ever since.' He slowed down as the edges of his lips turned upwards. 'My world.'

She didn't speak for a few seconds, just stared at him. 'That's how you came into research?'

He nodded. 'I was already in cardiology. But, you'll understand, the clinical side is tough.' He hadn't asked her for her reasons for leaving her clinical role, but he'd understood the implication. People who'd spent years training to be a doctor didn't walk away unless they had no real choice.

'It didn't work for me with no real help at home, covering emergencies and on calls with a baby. Research was the natural place. Find out what I needed to know, while still keeping a clinical role—in more manageable hours.'

She nodded as he continued. 'And with the potential for Rory...' He let his voice tail off.

The realisation didn't take long to hit her. She worked in research. She knew exactly what he was getting at. Cardiomyopathy was a hereditary condition.

'Rory has the gene?'

'Rory has the gene,' he repeated.

She didn't hesitate. She reached over and squeezed his hand. 'Oh, Gene. I'm so sorry.'

He drew in a deep breath. 'So am I. But that's life. You'll know the odds. He had a fifty per cent chance of inheriting the gene—and he has. But so far there are no symptoms. No indication that there's anything to worry about. That's what I need to keep inside my head. But it doesn't stop me making this my life's work.'

He didn't need to say any more. She'd know

thc potential. She'd know that hypertrophic cardiomyopathy was the condition frequently undetected then associated with young sportsmen suddenly dying.

That was why the 'no symptoms' was so important to keep in his head. Because late at night, when he looked at that gorgeous little mop of blond hair, every worst-case scenario in the world wound its way through his head.

Her voice had a sympathetic tone and he could see the understanding her eyes as she looked at him. 'So you're committed. You want to be here. You want to do the work.'

He could tell she was almost relieved. If he'd turned and walked out today because Professor Helier wasn't going to be around, it could have potentially brought the research to a halt. But he'd never do that. He repeated those words. 'I want to do the work. It's important to me. It's important to Rory. And it's important to a whole host of other people all around the world affected by this disease.' He didn't have a single doubt about what he was saying.

She gave a nod of approval and held her hand out towards the next wing. 'Well, in that case,

Dr Du Bois, come and meet your fabulous team. And your fabulous patients.'

Her head was swimming as she pasted a smile on her face. Her heart ached for him—literally.

Now she understood—probably a whole lot better than he expected her to.

The thought that his gorgeous little son could have a ticking time bomb in his chest—similar to her own—was heart-wrenching. How must it feel to look at that little guy every day and wonder if at some point he would develop symptoms or become unwell? As a medic, one thing was crystal clear in her head. Parents shouldn't outlive their kids. They just shouldn't. There was something so wrong about that. Unbearable. And she wasn't even a mother.

She'd worked with families who'd lost kids due to cardiac defects and anomalies and there was something so wrong about it all.

They walked down to the east wing—where all the patients were seen and monitored. The Rueben Institute was like many other cardiac research centres. They monitored patients with certain conditions, seeing if small lifestyle changes could have impacts on their lives, along with dietary changes and alternative therapies. They also monitored certain new medicines, making sure that patients didn't have any side effects and comparing the differences between them and the existing medicines. There was no point introducing a new medicine to the world if it didn't really make any improvements for patients.

There were similar institutes all over the world, but in the land of cardiac conditions, with or without any trials, patients' conditions could change in an instant. The staff here were highly trained and the institute well equipped to deal with any emergency. Cordelia showed him from room to room.

'We have twenty monitoring bays for the clinical trials. We also have overnight beds available with monitoring, too, for anyone feeling unwell.'

'Who covers that?'

Cordelia dabbed an electronic tablet next to one of the doors and grabbed hold of one his hands. She pulled up a page and pressed his forefinger to the pad, shooting him a smile. 'As quick as that—your fingerprint will open any of these. It gives a complete list of all patient details, contacts and staff on duty. At any time we have two doctors on—day and night—along with four nursing staff. We never fall under that ratio and are frequently above it.'

He frowned a little. 'Do those numbers include you and me?'

She shook her head. 'Oh, no. We're supernumerary—along with all the research staff. Around fifty per cent of our researchers have a clinical background. And working here helps them maintain their clinical registrations. You'll frequently see our researchers doing the clinical monitoring of patients.' She tried to choose her words carefully. 'Quite often, our clinicians have had to go into research because of health conditions of their own. Working here helps them still have the patient contact that they love, as well as contributing to improving things for patients.'

He nodded thoughtfully. 'So, what will be expected of me while Professor Helier isn't here?'

She tried not to pull a face, hoping that nothing she would say would make him bolt for the door. She really didn't know much about Gene Du Bois at all. He might seem like a stand-up guy, but some people couldn't handle pressure, and he might not like what came next.

'Professor Helier was very hands on. Every morning he would review every patient—usually around twenty, who would be involved in research in that day. The nursing staff would highlight any issues or concerns to him, and he might end up ordering cardiac echoes, ECGs, chest X-rays and listening to chests. He frequently adjusted medications for heart failure, arrhythmias, and so on. We do have protocols for all this,' she added quickly. 'You wouldn't be doing it blind.'

He gave a quick shake of his head and a wave of his hand. 'That all sounds fine. I like patient contact.' He gave a smile and raised his eyebrows. 'Some people might say I even crave it. Just a check, though—what if someone needs an intervention? Do we have links with a local hospital?'

Cordelia nodded and pulled up some more information on the tablet. 'Here's the contact details and private consultants we deal with. If, for some reason, someone had an aneurysm or needed a bypass, we have a red-button service with a private ambulance service here, and our patients would get seen right away.'

She looked at him warily. 'How long since your last cath lab session?'

He pulled back in surprise. 'Two weeks. Why?'

She frowned. It wasn't quite the answer she was expecting, even though she was secretly relieved. 'Why two weeks?'

He shrugged. 'I covered sessions for doctors on annual leave at my last job. It was all daytime, scheduled theatre time, so I didn't need cover for Rory. It worked out fine. Why?'

She smiled and led him to another door. 'Because we have our own cath lab here. It was built for emergencies but has been used on a number of occasions. Our own doctors are perfectly proficient, but it's best if you're up to date too. We also have an anaesthetist on call, and all our usual cardiac technicians are available whenever required.'

He stepped into the white cath lab. All the equipment was state of the art and practically sparkling. He walked around, taking slow steps, checking it out, running his fingers over the monitors before finally giving an approving nod. He opened a few drawers, looked where equipment was stored and then had a final check, familiarising himself with the contents of the cardiac arrest trolley. 'Emergency code?'

'Code red.' She pointed to a phone on the wall. 'Pick up any phone, say the words "Code red" and an announcement will come over the Tannoy. You don't even need to give your location. It automatically identifies where you are and gives the location in the call.'

He folded his arms as he turned to face Cordelia. 'Everything seems very well organised.'

'I hope that it is.'

He stepped a little closer. 'So, what will you be doing?'

She gave a nod. 'Overseeing the whole place. Dealing with the drug companies and investors. Meeting the Japanese investors due in a few days. All the while mirroring what you'll be doing here for cardiomyopathy in my own department for heart failure and heart regeneration studies. My clinics run in parallel with yours. We have two separate teams.' She rolled her eyes. 'And if I get half a chance, I might even clear Franc's desk.'

He laughed. 'Is it that bad?'

She shook her head as she led him back out of the cath lab. 'Oh, no. It's worse. Now, come along and I'll introduce you to your team. I'll warn you in advance. The secretary for the project, Marie, is the scariest, most organised, ruthlessly efficient human being you will ever meet.' She bent over and whispered in his ear. 'I think she might actually be a cyborg. But that's another story.'

He tipped his head back and let out a hearty laugh. It was the first she'd heard since he'd got there. Her insides had been churning for a little while, hoping he wouldn't say he didn't want to take over Professor Helier's clinical responsibilities. Not everyone would. But Gene Du Bois seemed completely comfortable. It was like water off a duck's back to him. She grinned as she pushed open another door.

'Don't let it be said we're not welcoming.' A delicious smell met them. 'This is the coffee lounge. Or the tea lounge. Or the natural fruit water lounge. Whatever your preference is—we'll have it. And if we don't? Let us know and we'll order it in. We like staff to be comfortable. And well nourished. If you have dietary requirements—or if Rory has dietary requirements in day care—just let the kitchen staff know. They aim to please.'

He looked around at the comfortable red sofas, the TVs mounted on walls, the work stations with computers, and the large white tables and chairs for dining.

Cordelia kept watching him. 'We like people to be comfortable,' she reiterated. 'Not everyone thrives in an office environment. Professor Helier doesn't care where people work—just as long as they do.'

Gene nodded in approval and put his hands on his hips. 'This sounds like a good work ethic. I could get comfortable here.' Little crinkles appeared around his eyes as he smiled and she felt a little warmth spread throughout her belly. He was happy. Good. She wanted things to go well while Professor Helier was away. The last thing she wanted to do was phone him with some kind of disaster.

Gene strolled over to a glass jar stuffed with tiny sweets wrapped in gold foil. 'And what are these? Some kind of treasure?'

She smiled as she joined him and stole one from the jar. 'Gene, you're in Switzerland. What are we famous for?'

He wrinkled his nose. 'Alps. And the Geneva Convention.'

She shook her head and rolled her eyes. 'You Americans. Chocolate, Gene. That's what Switzerland is famous for. Chocolate.'

She held up her little sweet and started to unwrap it. Within a few seconds the dreamy cocoa milky smell had reached them both. He even started to lean a little towards it.

His eyes started to glaze. 'Is this really a good idea for a place that specialises in cardiac research?'

She gave a broad smile. 'That's why they're tiny. Just enough to give you the magical sensation of chocolate hitting every taste bud, without sending your blood glucose spiralling and your weight out of control.' She gave her best intelligent nod. 'You know, research has proved that if you just take a little of what you crave, it makes management much easier.'

He made a grab for the chocolate. 'I'll take your word for it.'

For some reason, even though she wasn't entirely sure of Gene, there was something very amicable about him. She felt quite safe around him. And while that might not be what some guys would want to hear, it was important to her.

She was very used to erecting walls around herself. But, after his initial reaction of ignoring her question about Rory's mother, he'd told her—in his own time—what had actually happened. Most people probably felt sorry for him. He could easily take on the widower persona. But he didn't. Not at all. Instead, he'd been straight about his story. There had been no great love between him and Mindy. He hadn't even really had the chance to be angry with her. Cordelia didn't have a single doubt that most guys would have been totally blindsided by all of it.

But Gene seemed to have taken the news about his son well. He loved his son. And whilst she was sure he wished he could change his genetic heritage, he seemed to have accepted it for what it was.

She met a lot of patients who hated what their genes meant for them. Something they could never control. Her own were the same. And she'd long since known that accepting what you couldn't change was the biggest part of the process for some people.

Like her. Like Gene. And, eventually, hopefully like Rory.

She gave him a sideways glance as she led him down towards the offices for the clinics.

'Maybe I should have recommended that you take a handful of chocolates to get you through the next part of the day.'

He gave her a suspicious glance. 'What do you mean? Aren't I just reviewing the patients and taking care of the clinic work and trial?'

She licked her lips and gave a little sigh. 'You make it sound so simple.'

He stopped walking. 'Isn't it?'

She couldn't help herself. She winked at him as she reached the doors. 'Oh, Dr Du Bois, you have a lot to learn. Welcome to the Reuben Institute. Now, come and meet your master.'

Gene was sprawled across the sofa. Rory was also sprawled across him, sleeping, with his mouth open and drool landing on Gene's shirt. He hadn't even had a chance to change since they'd got home.

Cordelia appeared and took in the scene, leaning against the doorjamb and crossing her arms. At some point in the day she'd changed back into her red baseball boots. He couldn't get over quite how quirky and cute she looked with her business-style dress and jacket, coupled with flat red baseball boots.

'You survived?' she asked.

He raised his eyebrows and held out his hands. 'If I could jump off this sofa right now and chase you down, I would.'

She shook her head. 'That's fighting talk.'

He nodded. 'It is. But now I've met your lethal weapon—Marie.'

Cordelia couldn't pretend not to laugh. 'I did try to warn you.' Then she shook her head, 'And, oh, no. She's not mine. She's yours. I did tell you might need chocolate to see you through.'

'But you didn't tell me why,' he quipped.

She sighed and shook her head. 'No, I didn't. You'd just lulled me into what could be a false sense of security. You'd told me you would stay. I didn't want to frighten you off.'

'You just left that to Marie?'

Cordelia laughed again. 'What can I say? She's chewed up tougher guys than you.' She walked over and perched on the edge of the sofa, her eyes on the sleeping figure of Rory. 'I'm sorry. But Marie has been at the institute since the day it opened. She's almost like the institute herself. She knows every patient. Every trial. She has the scariest but most brilliant encyclopaedic brain in the world.'

He nodded. 'She certainly doesn't let anyone get around her.'

Cordelia nodded. 'And it's not worth the energy even trying. And whatever you do—don't use her mug. It's the one thing that will absolutely tip her over the edge.'

He wrinkled his brow. 'Seriously?'

She nodded. 'Completely.'

'Then thanks for the warning. What mug is hers?' She could see him picturing the jam-packed cabinet in the staff kitchen.

'Why, Dr Du Bois, couldn't you tell just by looking?'

He narrowed his gaze. 'I'm going to like this, aren't I?'

She nodded again. 'It's Glinda. The Good Witch from the *Wizard of Oz*.'

His shoulders started to shake and he lifted his hand to the sleeping Rory on his chest, trying not to disturb him. 'No way. It should be Darth Vader, or at the very least the Wicked Witch.'

Cordelia smiled. He seemed to have settled. On a few occasions she had actually been worried that Marie might chase some of the visiting doctors away. Her manner was...brusque, to say the least.

'I agree. Now, what would you like for dinner?'

He placed his hands on Rory's back and swung his legs around so he was finally sitting up on the sofa. 'It's my turn to sort out dinner—you bought pizza last night.'

'But you've got your hands full.'

He shook his head. 'But that doesn't mean I can't take a turn.' He looked down and gave Rory a little shake. 'He's worn out from day care today. But, thankfully, he loved it.'

'That's great. I thought he would.'

He nodded again. 'And you'll see the hire company dropped off a car for me so you don't need to ferry us around. I didn't want to be an extra burden to you this month when you have an institute to run.'

She waved her hand. 'It was fine. It was no problem.' But secretly it was. She was glad he'd been thoughtful enough to hire a car. It meant she could head in early to the institute, or stay late if she needed to.

He looked up. 'Why don't you let me get changed and I'll take us all to dinner. I'll drive. You can suggest somewhere that suits.'

She looked down at her baseball boots. 'I should change too. Shouldn't really go any-where dressed like this.'

'Don't. You look great.' It came just a little too easily and she felt heat rush into her cheeks.

Rory started to wake up. 'I'm hungry,' he murmured.

Gene set him down on the floor. 'Then it's decided. Let's go for dinner. And...' he gave Cordelia a cheeky smile '...I may even tell you how I plan to conquer the mountain that is Marie.'

An hour later he was dressed in jeans and a T-shirt and sitting in one of the local restaurants that Cordelia had recommended. 'The staff are great and there's a good kids' menu. It always seems to be full of families.'

That was recommendation enough for him and the service was quick.

She hadn't changed. She'd kept on her red dress and her baseball boots. And even though he noticed a few raised eyebrows, Cordelia seemed immune to them. She was comfortable in her own skin. He liked that about her.

He could tell she was still a little wary around Rory. But that was fine. She didn't have any kids of her own and some people just weren't natural around kids. It wasn't as if she ignored him. Or didn't bother. It was just he could almost sense her nerves. They almost seemed to jangle when she had to interact with the little boy.

It almost felt as if there was something he just couldn't put his finger on.

But tonight things were fine. They'd eaten dinner and, as he'd offered to drive, Cordelia had drunk a glass of wine. As they waited for Rory to eat his ice cream, he gave her a nod. 'I know how to win her around.'

She wrinkled her nose. 'Who?'

'Marie.'

He could tell she was instantly amused. Marie was a hard nut to crack. From what he'd heard, Marie had broken more than a few researchers who'd dared to challenge her on something.

She folded her arms across her chest. 'And how, exactly, are you going to win Marie around? Tell me. I'm fascinated.'

His eyes twinkled. 'It's simple really. She loves my accent. She's told me more than once.'

'But that still doesn't mean she likes you.' She ran her fingers up and down the stem of the wine glass.

He gave a conciliatory nod. 'No, it doesn't. But she will.'

Now she looked really intrigued. 'How?'

'I have a secret weapon.'

For a second she didn't say anything but her eyes rested on Rory, who was busy almost examining the bottom of his ice-cream bowl to make sure he hadn't missed any ice cream. 'Is that fair?' The tone of her voice was a little strange.

He didn't push her on the tone. He just leaned back in his chair. 'I'm bringing out my secret weapon. I'm going to go full cowboy on her.'

'What?' Several people in the restaurant turned around at the rise in her voice.

He laughed 'Yip. I'm wearing my Stetson tomorrow. Probably the boots, maybe even the jeans. What do you think?'

'You're serious?' She had the strangest expression on her face.

He leaned forward a little, catching a whiff of her orange-scented perfume. 'Of course I'm serious. What did you think I meant?'

She gave a little shrug but she didn't meet his gaze. 'Oh, I don't know. I thought you might have been using Rory.' She pointed across the table. 'I mean, one look at his gorgeous little face and…'

Gene followed her gaze across the table, where by this point Rory had ice cream on his face, his hands and his T-shirt. But you'd never know, because he was still concentrating so completely on the tiniest bit of ice cream at the bottom of the bowl.

'Everyone's a sucker,' he finished for her.

His heart squeezed. Even though she wasn't that easy around Rory it was clear she could see the appeal that made him thankful every single day that he'd found this little boy.

He turned to Rory and lifted the bowl away from him. 'Give me that before you start licking the bowl.' He wiped Rory's face and hands with a napkin. 'Time to go home, champ.' He raised his fist and Rory bumped his against his dad's.

'What is that?' asked Cordelia.

'The fist bump? That's just us. That's our move.'

'Your move?'

Rory wriggled out of his seat and Gene followed, picking up the bill from the table. 'You know, everyone has a move, or a saying, something like that.'

She put her hands on her hips. 'They do?'

He nodded. 'Of course. Don't you?'

She frowned for a second. 'I don't think so.'

He nodded as he settled the bill. 'Leave it with me. I bet you've got one. I'll figure it out.'

They walked out to the car and Gene strapped Rory in before making a grab for something in the back seat before Cordelia had even managed to climb in.

His Stetson. He plonked it on his head with a cheeky wink. 'Is that fair? Going full cowboy on her? Like I said, I'll even wear my boots and jeans if you think it will help.'

Cordelia laughed out loud. 'You really are going to wear that to the institute tomorrow?'

He tipped his Stetson towards her. 'I told you, it's my lethal weapon.'

He watched her suck in a breath as his eyes connected with hers. He was joking. Of course he was joking. So why had his heart rate just quickened? Ridiculous. It was like being a teenager again.

He shook his head as he took off his Stetson

and climbed back into the car. He was only here for a month. He had work to do. And a child to look after. He couldn't afford any distractions.

But as Cordelia hitched up her dress to climb into the car, he had a distinct flash of toned, tanned leg.

And try as he may, he couldn't get it out of his head on the drive home.

CHAPTER THREE

CORDELIA SIGHED AND leaned against the wall as she checked the chart again. One of her patients was failing. Truth was, most of the patients in the heart failure study were failing—that was why they were here.

But Jonas Delphine was one of her favourites. He was an old sea captain, eighty-six, and had smoked for forty years. His chest complaints, along with his cardiovascular disease and heart failure, made him a difficult candidate to manage.

Some trials only wanted 'perfect' candidates. Ones who had no other health complaints but who had unhealthy lifestyle issues that could be changed and monitored then assessed to within an inch of their lives. But the Reuben Institute didn't work with unrealistic patients. What was the point of that? More complicated patients meant more bias for the trials. Some people didn't like that. Some drug companies definitely didn't like it. But Professor Helier had always been clear. The institute was here to help *real* patients. Not perfect ones who didn't really exist.

Now, after listening to Jonas's heart and lungs, she'd just ordered another chest X-ray and echo cardiogram.

'Something wrong?' Gene's voice made her jump.

She couldn't help but grin at the sight of him. He'd been a man of his word and had come to the institute this morning full cowboy.

The patients loved it. The staff loved it. The Stetson, cowboy boots and jeans had certainly made their mark. Even the normally frosty Marie had seemed to like his unusual appearance.

Gene was still wearing his Stetson and tipped it towards her. 'Cordelia?'

She held up the electronic tablet. 'Nothing that a new heart won't cure.' She straightened up. 'Actually, now that you're here, you can give me a second opinion on someone.'

He held up his electronic tablet. 'Great minds

think alike. I was just coming to get you to do the same.'

A tiny surge of pride welled in her stomach. She was pleased. Pleased that he'd came to her for a second opinion on one of his patients. Hopefully, that meant he thought she might be a good clinician.

They swapped tablets. 'You tell me yours, and I'll tell you mine.'

'Aryssa Maia, forty-seven, hypertrophic cardiomyopathy. She's had unsuccessful ablations for atrial fibrillation and she can't tolerate the usual drugs. She also has a permanent pacemaker in place. I've checked her previous scans and just listened to her chest. I think her ventricle is getting to the stage it is barely functioning. She's symptomatic, breathless and tired, with swollen extremities.'

She nodded. 'I have a similar case. Jonas Delphine is eighty-six, with existing COPD and chronic heart failure. I think I'm going to have to take him off the study and put him on IV steroids and diuretics. In the space of one day he's gone downhill fast.'

Gene nodded slowly. She knew he understood.

The patient's welfare was always their prime concern. But the regulations for any research study were strict. They didn't want any findings skewed. If they used certain other drugs on patients then they were taken off the study programme. It was important that any improvement in a patient's current condition was only attributed to the drug being studied—not to any other intervention made.

Cordelia sighed as she looked at Aryssa's chart. 'She was doing so well,' she said sadly. 'I really thought that this might be the one drug that could make a difference for her.'

Gene ran his fingers through his hair. 'I get that. But my gut is telling me that something else is going on. I almost feel as if her pacing wire has moved. Her heart just isn't functioning the way it should be.'

He glanced at Jonas's chart and smiled. 'Why do I feel as if this guy could teach me everything I need to know about life?'

'He probably could. I'm not ashamed to say I love him and have a completely unnatural bias towards him.' She lifted her hand. 'That's why I'm checking for a second opinion. I need someone who can just look at the clinical signs.' She gave a slow nod and handed back Aryssa's notes. 'And as for your patient, I agree, she needs an ECG and a cardiac echo. I suspect her pacing wire has moved too. That's what fits the symptoms, rather than anything happening within the trial.'

He gave a nod. 'I ordered the tests. Just wanted to double check.' He kept a hold of Jonas's tablet. 'Now, let's go meet your patient, while mine has her investigations.'

Things moved so swiftly here. He was secretly pleased that Cordelia had come to him for a second opinion. By the time he'd sounded Jonas's chest and looked at his hands and ankles, the nurse from his part of the clinic had brought along Aryssa's ECG. It couldn't be clearer. The pacing wire definitely wasn't capturing, meaning Aryssa's heart rate was erratic and low. Both he and Cordelia nodded.

'I'll come back and speak to her. But can you attach her to a portable cardiac monitor in the meantime and ask them to put a rush on that cardiac echo?'

The nurse gave a nod. 'I'll take her for the echo now.'

He gave Cordelia a nod and walked through to the treatment room. 'It looks like we're both about to lose patients from our trials. Jonas needs some IV steroids and diuretics.'

Her eyes were downcast for a moment. It probably wasn't what she wanted to hear. But he knew she would always put the patients first. That's the way it should be. Research work always brought these challenges and any medic who worked on the trials knew that.

She looked back up, nodding and opening the drug cupboard. 'I'll draw them up. Can you prescribe them on the tablet? Thanks.'

He gave her a nod and checked the bottles with her as she drew up the medicines. He couldn't pretend not to notice the slight shake of her hands. 'How about I do this for you? You can distract Jonas and persuade him this is a good idea.'

She sucked in a deep breath and let her hands rest back down on the counter top. 'Do you know what? I'd like that. Thank you.' She gave him a small smile and his insides clenched. He got the distinct impression that Cordelia Greenway didn't normally let anyone help her. But from the way her jaw had been clenched and the shake in her hands he knew she was emotional about this. He knew she felt connected to this old guy. She'd worked here for four years. She might even have known him that long.

It was hard not to get attached to patients you saw on a regular basis, let alone nearly every day. It was harder still if those patients condition got worse—which inevitably frequently happened to doctors.

He understood. He'd been there and felt it himself. For the last few years he'd moved from place to place. All of his emotional investment had been in Rory. That's the way it had to be. He'd had to learn to be mom and dad to the little guy. He'd always done a good job by his patients, but he hadn't been around long enough to form lasting relationships.

And he missed that. He couldn't pretend that he didn't.

He moved his hand to lift the tray with the syringe and Venflon but Cordelia's was still there. His first instinct was to pull away, but instead he put his hand over hers and left it there as she gave a little sad sigh.

She didn't object. She didn't jerk away. The heat of her hand filled his palm in a way he hadn't expected.

It had been a long time since he'd touched a woman—held a woman. Of course he touched patients every day. But relationships in the last three years just hadn't been possible. He didn't want to be the guy who introduced Rory to a new girlfriend every few months so it had been easier just to let that part of his life slide.

So…this was different. Not new exactly, but just different. And up until this moment he hadn't realised how much he'd missed connecting with someone.

She gave the briefest nod of her head and he knew it was time to pull away. He lifted his hand and let hers slide out from underneath his, picked up the tray, and gave her a conciliatory nod. 'Let's go and make Jonas feel better.'

It was the little things that made you realise how thoughtful someone could be. Her insides had twisted and turned at the thought of being the person who would deliver the treatment to end Jonas's time on the trial. She knew it was essential. She knew it was the right thing to do. But part of her had ached, knowing she would have to be the one to do it.

The thought of not seeing him five days a week made her sad. After four years she was sure Jonas still had a world of stories to tell her. His cheery nature in the face of his heart failure made her feel more positive about her own condition.

She had to have hope. She had to feel as if one day her Wolff-Parkinson-White syndrome wouldn't cause some odd arrhythmia that would send her heart into a whole host of problems. For some people with her condition it could lead to death.

Five years ago her physician had sat her down and given her the news she'd known would be coming. She should look at a permanent contraception choice. Her Wolff-Parkinson–White syndrome was progressing. Her condition was unpredictable. What was certain was that the extra stress and increase in pressure of a pregnancy would cause huge strain on her already struggling heart. Pregnancy was out of the question. She'd never have a family of her own.

She'd been living with a fellow researcher then. Han. They'd been working together in London and their relationship had just developed slowly. She'd liked that. He'd known about her condition and had helped her through difficult spells.

But the news from the consultant had been a turning point. Han had backed off, slowly but surely. Never with malice. But his plans for the future included a family. And as he'd drifted away she'd felt more and more hurt. More and more like less of a woman. Less of a partner.

She'd had to learn to accept that a family wouldn't be in her future. She'd had to accept that any potential relationship would have to be one where she had that difficult up-front conversation. The one where she'd have to admit she was unsure what the future with her cardiac condition would look like.

In the meantime, she'd thrown herself into work. Her almost safe place. But every now and then, when a patient's condition worsened at the clinic, it always brought home to her the fact that one day that could be her.

So she was grateful to Gene for the offer. And he'd been true to his word. He'd charmed Jonas and given him time to express his sadness at having to leave the trial before graciously accepting the other treatment that he needed. Gene kept him distracted with cowboy-type stories as he slowly administered the medicine to Jonas.

They'd just finished up when one of the other nurses came rushing in. 'Dr Du Bois? We need you now. Aryssa has become unwell during her cardiac echo.'

Both of them moved at once, walking down the long white corridor rapidly. Gene reached the room first. He moved swiftly around Aryssa and examined her, taking in her vital signs. 'She's bradycardic,' said Cordelia, moving to the other side of the bed.

The sonographer was pale-faced next to the bed. 'She just seemed to fade while we were doing the echo,' he said.

'What did it show?' asked Gene.

The sonographer gave him a serious look.

'What you expected. The pacing wire has moved.'

Gene frowned as Aryssa's eyes flickered open. 'It's odd. That's unusual. A pacing wire shouldn't move.'

Cordelia put her hand on Aryssa's shoulder. 'Aryssa, how are you feeling?'

The heart rate on the monitor seemed to rise for a few seconds. 'Not good,' she whispered.

Cordelia nodded. 'Don't worry. We'll look after you. But has anything happened in the last day or so that could have dislodged your pacing wire?'

Aryssa lifted her hand to her chest. 'I had an accident in the car on the way to the institute this morning. It was only a small bump, but the airbag exploded.'

Gene shot Cordelia a look. 'Did the airbag hit you?'

Aryssa winced. 'Yes. But I got more of a fright because of the noise. And the powder.' She closed her eyes again, obviously exhausted just answering those few questions.

They moved outside into the corridor.

Gene didn't hesitate. 'That's enough for me.

We need to insert a new pacing wire. She's too symptomatic to move her elsewhere.'

It was the weirdest feeling. All of a sudden she almost felt as if she were a spectator instead of part of the situation. As if she were dangling up somewhere in the corner of the room, watching everything.

She couldn't remember the last time there had been an emergency in the clinic. Not like this anyway.

Everything she'd ever learned at medical school decided to fly out of her head in an instant. She couldn't tell a clavicle from a femur, or an atrium from a liver lobe.

Crap. She'd never panicked as a medical student. She'd always been one of the calmest in the class. While others had fainted at the sight of blood, or any other body fluid, Cordelia had just wondered why on earth they wanted to be doctors.

So what was wrong with her now?

One of the clinic nurses appeared at her side. 'Are we pacing?'

Simple words. And that was all it took. Her brain shifted gear.

Gene walked into the next-door cath lab. His actions were automatic. It was clear he'd dealt with this situation before. He pulled over a trolley and set out the equipment. He nodded to the nurse. 'Can you bring the patient in, please, and we'll explain what we need to do.'

Cordelia moved over to the sink and started scrubbing her hands. A temporary pacing wire wasn't performed in a traditional operating theatre, but the cath lab was as good as it got around here. The wire went straight into a central vein, and everything had to be done aseptically to protect the patient from infection.

The nurse wheeled Aryssa in. She was lying on her back, her face pale and sweating. She was already attached to a portable cardiac monitor showing her very slow heartbeat and low blood pressure.

Gene gave Cordelia a nod. He moved over and took Aryssa's hand. He mouthed one word to her. 'Cold.'

Cordelia pressed her lips together. Cold extremities meant that the blood flow just wasn't getting enough power to circulate properly. She dried her hands and held them out in front of her to where the nurse was holding out a disposable surgical gown. Next came the gloves then she checked the equipment on the trolley.

'Percutaneous sheath, bipolar pacing catheter and bridging cables and pacing box.' She murmured the contents out loud, mentally ticking them off in her head.

Gene spoke quietly to Aryssa. 'Aryssa, I know you might be feeling light-headed. We're sure that your pacing wire has moved. We're going to insert a temporary pacing line to get your heart back on track. You'll probably be a little woozy until we get this sorted. But trust us. We've got this.'

Aryssa's eyes were closed but she tossed her head from side to side. 'But I'll be flung off the trial. I don't want that. The drug is the only thing that's worked for me.'

Gene met Cordelia's gaze. Her heart gave a little flutter inside her chest and that made her freeze. *Oh, no. Not now. Not here.*

He spoke smoothly. 'Aryssa, with a heartbeat of around forty we couldn't let you stay in the trial. We've got to keep you healthy. This isn't something we can debate. You need this procedure.'

A tear trickled down Aryssa's cheek and Gene clasped her hand tightly while looking at Cordelia. It was awful. Aryssa had been doing so well on the trial. The new drug seemed to be having a good effect on her. Her symptoms had diminished over the last few weeks and up until the last day her heart function had looked a little better.

Hypertrophic cardiomyopathy could throw up a whole host of problems, depending on which part of the heart was most affected. Right now, they had no way of reversing the condition, but this drug had actually looked as though it could slow and stabilise the condition, optimising the output of the heart.

Gene looked so conflicted. She could almost see what he was seeing—Rory on the bed instead of Aryssa. It must be breaking his heart.

For a few seconds his dark brown gaze intersected with hers. He wasn't a doctor right now, he was a parent. It was like seeing the window to his soul. His hopes and fears all tumbling over and over. She gave him the briefest nod of acknowledgement and it was almost like flicking a switch.

His doctor face fell back into place.

'What site?' asked Gene.

Cordelia breathed deeply, focused and ran her eyes over her patient as the sonographer appeared. She gave him a grateful smile and a nod as he moved into position without even speaking.

She looked at Aryssa's neck. There was a small white scar at her neck—obviously the place of the last insertion. The right internal jugular vein was the preferred option due to the ease of positioning the wire into the right ventricle. But since it had already been used there was a risk of scar tissue. She wanted this procedure to go smoothly.

She could see Gene's eyes following hers. 'Looks like the left subclavian is our best option,' she said.

The nurse gave a nod and eased Aryssa's gown down from her left shoulder, giving easy access to her left clavicle and covering around the area with sterile drapes. Cordelia picked up a swab and cleansed the area, feeling with her fingers for the identifying features. She then nodded to the sonographer, who placed his probe just under the clavicle, allowing her to identify the artery and vein on the screen. As the artery and vein were so close it was important to familiarise herself with the patient's anatomy.

She waited until the arterial wave form was shown, to differentiate between the artery and vein, then injected some local anaesthetic into the site.

Gene's voice was low and reassuring in the background. He talked to Aryssa the whole time she lay with her eyes closed, keeping a soft grip of her hand.

Cordelia threaded the dilator into the catheter, attaching it to the needle and inserting it, waiting for the flash of blood, before continuing. She held the needle steady while advancing the wire into the vein. She then removed the needle, made a little cut with the scalpel and inserted the sheath, with the dilator in place, over the wire.

'Almost done,' she said quietly to Aryssa.

'I'm just removing the wire and testing the balloon on the pacing wire.' That only took a few minutes then she completed the procedure by inserting the wire into Aryssa. The wire was attached to the pacing box and it turned on. They watched on the screen as the balloon allowed the wire to be positioned. A few seconds later the pacing spikes appeared on the monitor, showing them that the wire was in the correct position.

Cordelia still marvelled at the technology they had these days that allowed them to do relatively complicated procedures in such a quiet and controlled environment. They waited another few minutes, watching the monitor for any potential changes. It only took a few seconds for Gene to smile and nod and for Aryssa's cheeks to start to pink up. Her heart rate was now sitting at around seventy beats per minute. The pacing wire was doing its job.

They held steady. Waiting to ensure that everything was in place.

That was when it started. The noise like horses'

hooves in her ears. That feeling of a runaway train in her chest.

No. Please, no.

She stared down at her gloved hands, wanting to lift one to her neck. But she couldn't. This was a sterile procedure.

She tried to take some long, slow, steadying breaths. But it was useless. She knew that. She'd dealt with this condition too long.

She kept her voice as steady as it could be. 'Dr Du Bois, would it be possible for you to stitch the line in place for me, please?'

The nurse next to her turned her head in surprise, and Gene looked up. He gave her the strangest look. Stitching only took a matter of minutes—minutes that she didn't feel like she had right now. It seemed odd to ask another doctor to scrub and get sterile. It would take him longer to do that than it would for her to do the stitching. But her head was starting to swim. She had to get out of here. Now.

She didn't wait for his answer. She just turned to the nurse next to her, who was already gowned and wearing sterile gloves. 'Could you hold this for me until Dr Du Bois is ready, please? I need to get a little air.'

The nurse moved swiftly, sliding her hands over Cordelia's so there was no change in position. Cordelia didn't hesitate. She turned and left as the thudding in her chest threatened to overtake her. She heard someone call her name. But she couldn't afford to wait.

Her legs were shaking almost as much as her head. Heat swamped her and she tugged the sterile gown from her throat and sterile gloves from her hands as she staggered the last few steps to her office.

It was like a sanctuary. She didn't even have time to close the door but slid down the wall, automatically putting her fingers to her neck to start massaging.

It was all she could think about. All she could concentrate on. Every molecule in her body had to think about those fingers. It was her own fault. She'd never left it this long before. She always dealt with the arrhythmia as soon as she'd felt it. As soon as she'd had symptoms.

She counted in her head. Slowly. One...two... three. It was impossible. Counting wouldn't slow her heart rate. Or stop the wooziness in her head. Or the tightness in her chest.

She pictured something else. Green meadows. For as far as the eye could see. Flat green meadows. Dotted with daisies and dandelions. She sucked in a long, slow breath.

This was the place she liked to see when she needed to. It normally helped to centre her. Keep her calm. Keep her feeling in control, even though her body revolted. But this time there was a difference. This time something else was in *her* place. A blond-haired kid. And a broad-chested father. Smiling, laughing together. The father picking the kid up and swinging him in the air and the little guy screaming with joy.

It startled her. She'd never visualised things like this before. Her hands slid from her neck.

Her heart rate had slowed and she hadn't even noticed. She put her fingers on her wrist and counted her pulse. Old-fashioned but effective.

She let her head sag back against the wall. The tightness in her chest eased. Thank goodness. She pulled her shirt from her body. Cold sweat was uncomfortable. She'd need to change. Just as soon as she checked on Aryssa.

Her stomach clenched.

Patient. She had to check on her patient.

Gene was dumbfounded. Had she really just left?

The nurse met his gaze. 'She was paler than Aryssa,' she whispered in a voice only he could hear.

He nodded and swapped sides, moving to the sink to scrub. Another nurse appeared, holding out a disposable gown for him. Within a matter of minutes he was scrubbed and gloved and talking away to a much more alert Aryssa as he placed a couple of stitches to hold the pacing wire in situ.

If the rest of the staff thought it strange that Cordelia had left in mid-procedure they didn't say anything. But she hadn't really left in mid-procedure. He was being hard on her. She'd completed about ninety per cent before she'd bailed. But it still didn't make him feel any easier.

He kept talking, finished up, all the while

keeping an eye on Aryssa's ECG readouts before asking the nurse to keep her on the monitor for the next few hours. It was routine after a
procedure like this and Aryssa already looked
better. They would transfer her to another fa-
cility later. The pacing wire was only a temporary measure. She'd need a new permanent
pacemaker in the next few days.

She reached over and touched his arm. 'Thank
you, Dr Du Bois. I feel much better. But I can't
pretend to be happy about getting flung off the
trial. I'd finally found a drug that had actually
improved my other systems, and probably my
heart function. I feel as if—even though you've
given me a new pacing wire—it will go downhill from here. I'll miss the effects of that drug.'

He understood exactly what she was saying.
'Cardiomyopathy is a complicated disease. Even
when you have the gene, things can be different for every patient. You think the drug might
already have helped. And those effects might
last.'

Aryssa shook her head sadly. 'I don't think
so, Doc.' She sighed and leaned her head back
against the pillows. 'I'm just sorry this hap-

pened. All because some stray cat ran on the road in front of us.'

He wanted to tell her she could stay on the trial. He wanted to tell her there was a way around this. She'd had a pacing wire from the start. Who needed to know it had been replaced?

But Gene was far too ethical for that. The trial conditions had to be strictly adhered to. Trials were always strict—for good reason. They had to be absolutely crystal clear that any side effects or changes in a patient's condition were caused by the new trial drug and not by anything else.

He put his hand over Aryssa's. 'I'm sorry, Aryssa. You know there's nothing we can do about the rules of the trial. We have to follow them.'

A million thoughts were racing through his brain. This could be a drug that could help thousands of cardiomyopathy sufferers throughout the world. This could be the drug that could one day make a difference for his child.

He had to push all his personal feelings aside and think purely like a doctor, purely like a researcher. It was like being a coin, balancing on its edge. One tiny push could see him campaigning to keep Aryssa on the trial. And even though every professional bone in his body knew that was the wrong thing to do, the parent in him would always wonder if he should.

Aryssa was wheeled out to Recovery and Gene pulled off his gown and washed his hands again, running his fingers through his hair.

Cordelia. He had to find her. He had to ask her what on earth was going on.

He walked down the corridor towards her office, trying to play down the whole host of emotions currently circulating in his head. She was standing in front of the mirror, pulling her hair back into a ponytail. It looked a little damp. And she'd changed. She was wearing a green shirt instead of a pink one.

'Everything okay?'

She jumped at the sound of his voice, spun around to face him and glanced down, pulling at her shirt to straighten it.

'Have you quite finished titivating yourself?' He wasn't quite sure where the words had come from.

Her face fell, then he saw a sweep of anger

flare in her eyes. 'Titivating myself? Is that what you think I'm doing?'

It had been a poor choice of words. He knew that. But now he'd started, it seemed like he couldn't stop. It was almost as if his mouth went into overdrive. 'Well, what *are* you doing? You were in the middle of a procedure on a patient. I had to finish for you. I think I have a right to know.'

A scowl creased her face. Her reaction was immediate. 'No. You don't have any right to know anything. The pacing wire was in place and Aryssa's heart rate had improved. I stepped out because I felt unwell for a second. That's all. I got changed because I was uncomfortable.'

It was a plausible enough explanation. But for some reason he just didn't buy it. He was an experienced doctor. He knew when someone was hiding something from him. And that's exactly how he felt.

She took a deep breath. 'How is Aryssa? I was just about to come and see her.'

He spoke carefully, trying to maintain a hint of the composure that had already slipped. 'She's fine. I completed the stitches and she's in Recovery. She is still upset that she can't stay on the trial—just like Jonas was.'

Cordelia nodded solemnly. 'I'll talk to them both.'

'Shouldn't you sit down or something if you didn't feel well? Maybe you should eat something. Or drink something.' It was snappy. He knew that. But he also sensed she wasn't being up front.

She paused for a second. And he knew she was searching for something to say. It made his insides coil. Cordelia didn't strike him as someone who would be untruthful. And if she wasn't being untruthful? Then she was definitely hiding something from him.

'I'm fine,' she said quickly. 'I feel better now.'

He couldn't help himself. 'So quickly?'

She nodded and picked up some papers from her desk. 'Yes. Thank you for finishing up the procedure on Aryssa. I appreciate it. Now, if you'll excuse me, I have some work to do.'

She gave him a smile.

And somehow he knew she was resisting the temptation to say, 'As do you.'

She was second in command at the institute and he'd do well to remember that.

She swept past and strode down the corridor in front of him and he couldn't help but watch.

What did a woman like Cordelia Greenway have to hide—and why did he care?

CHAPTER FOUR

SHE'D JUST FINISHED pulling on her pyjamas when her bedroom door opened.

A little mop of blond hair appeared at the edge of the door. 'Rory? Is something wrong?'

'Want some milk,' he murmured.

She looked behind him. Gene wasn't in the corridor. 'Where's your dad?' she asked.

'He's in the shower. But I want some milk.' Rory walked tentatively into her room, holding a dog-eared book in one hand.

'Okay.' She nodded. 'I can get you some milk.' She looked at his bare feet. She wasn't quite sure where his slippers were, and didn't want to go into Gene's room to find them. Things had been a little tense for the last few days since the incident at the institute. He'd clearly been annoyed with her when he'd come to speak to her afterwards. She'd tried to make excuses but somehow she knew he hadn't really believed her.

Gene Du Bois was curious. He didn't like being fobbed off, and that's exactly what she'd tried to do.

It felt like they'd spent the last few days purposely avoiding each other and staying out of each other's way. It was almost like some carefully choreographed dance—but, then, she hadn't danced since she'd been a teenager and she'd no intention of starting again now.

She lifted Rory up onto her bed. 'Why don't you sit here for a minute while I go downstairs and get you some milk?'

'Okay,' he said, as he sat on her bed and looked around the room. She almost laughed out loud. Somewhere inside this four-year-old was a little old man waiting to get out. She could see him eyeing the clothes she'd thrown across a chair and her two pairs of shoes lying in one corner of the room.

Thankfully they had plenty of cold milk in the fridge downstairs so she poured some into a mug and carried it back up with her.

She walked around to the other side of the bed and climbed up alongside him, handing him the mug and praying he wouldn't spill it.

'I like your pyjamas,' he said as he took a sip of milk.

Her light jersey nightwear was bright pink and covered in tiny teddies. 'Thanks very much. I like yours too. Are they space rockets?'

He nodded. 'And planets. I was going to be an astronaut. But Dad says I might not be able to do that. So I'm going to be the scientist that presses the buttons and sends the shuttle into space.'

Her skin prickled. He was just a little guy but his vocabulary was so good. And his comprehension. But just because he sounded older than he was, it made her a little wary.

'You know, I think they get thousands of people who apply for every job as an astronaut. It's tough.'

He shrugged. 'I don't care. I'd get through.'

He said it with the confidence that only a child could have. She liked that. She wished she still had that herself. The fearlessness. The expectations.

Nowadays, if you could bottle and sell something like that you would be a millionaire.

She lay back on the bed and looked out at

the dark night sky. She hadn't remembered to close the curtains yet. She pointed up at the stars. 'Don't you think it might be a bit lonely up there?'

Her heart was giving a few little flutters in her chest. Not because anything was wrong but because somewhere along the line she figured that Gene must have had that general conversation with his little boy about doing certain things and getting certain jobs.

Hypertrophic cardiomyopathy was a tricky disease. The advice frequently said that children and adolescents with HCM should refrain from competitive high-activity sports to prevent the risk of sudden death.

Anyone with the HCM genes would never get on the space programme. Never be a deep-sea diver. Never be able to do certain other jobs. But did Gene really need to tell his kid that now?

She turned to face Rory as he took another sip of milk. 'But I wouldn't be lonely up there.'

'Why not?'

'Because my mom's up there.'

Her breath caught somewhere in the back of her throat. From the mouth of babes. She opened her mouth to speak but he kept talking, 'And I would take my girlfriend with me too. She's new. I met her today.'

Cordelia's brain was still dealing with the first statement. But she couldn't help but smile at the second. 'You have a girlfriend already? Who is she?'

He looked at Cordelia in surprise. 'I always have a girlfriend. Her name is Jana.'

Cordelia knew a lot of kids in the nursery and she frantically tried to remember which one was Jana.

'Blonde hair? Curls?'

Rory gave her a wide smile. 'That's her.'

'You've only been at nursery for a week and you've got a girlfriend already?'

He wrinkled his nose. 'Don't you have a boy-friend?'

She felt herself blushing. 'No. Not right now.' She gave a casual wave of her hand. 'Boys are too much trouble.' Then she rolled her eyes. 'And too messy.'

His dark brown eyes looked between her, her untidy pile of clothes, then back at her again. He didn't even have to say the words out loud.

Cordelia decided it was time for a quick subject change. 'Do you think your girlfriend wants to be an astronaut?'

Rory took another sip of milk and nodded his head thoughtfully. 'I'm not sure. Didn't you want to be an astronaut?'

She loved the way he asked her. As if every person on the planet wanted that job. She shook her head. 'Nope. I want to explore the pyramids. Or build a pirate ship and paint it red. Whatever came first.'

Something swept over his little face. 'Is that where your mom is?'

She almost felt her heart fold over in her chest. She couldn't help herself and did the most natural thing in the world. She sat up and put her arm around Rory's shoulder. 'No, honey. I'm very lucky. My mom is still here. She's quite old, but she lives by herself now.'

His brow creased and he looked up at her. 'Oh. My dad doesn't have his mommy any more, and neither do I.'

She wasn't used to kids. And she wasn't quite sure how to frame her reply. She'd had lots of life and death conversations with patients over the years—and with grief-stricken relatives. But this was a kid. Way out of her range of expertise.

'I heard that. And I'm sorry. But you've got a great dad. And I bet he does everything with you that a mom and a dad would do.'

Rory seemed to think for a few seconds then took another big glug of milk, resulting in the cutest milk moustache she'd ever seen.

This little guy could tear the heart clean out of her chest. It didn't matter that she felt as if she were treading on eggshells. It didn't matter she was so far out of her comfort zone it was scary. He had a way about him. An aura that just pulled her straight in.

'I might get a new mommy one day.'

She swallowed and spoke carefully. 'You might.'

His wide brown eyes looked up at her. 'Do you think she'll like me?'

She pulled him up on to her lap. 'Rory Du Bois, I think anyone who could be a mommy to you would consider herself the luckiest woman on the planet. Of course she'll like you. She won't just like you. She'll love you. Just as much as she loves your dad. That's how these things work. Your dad wouldn't marry anyone who didn't love you just as much as he does.'

She was probably way overstepping here. But even knowing Gene for a few days made her know that would be true.

Rory's big brown eyes were fixed on hers. He blinked. Just once, and put his head back down, leaning on her shoulder. 'That's okay, then,' he murmured.

She reached over and picked up the picture book. Strangely enough, it had a picture of a space rocket on the front cover. 'Want me to read this to you?' she asked.

Rory nodded and climbed off her lap and settled himself back under her arm. She didn't even want to acknowledge how that made her feel. The way that a tiny part of her that been tightly coiled up in her stomach for so long was slowly starting to unravel.

Or the fact that it made her realise just how much she was missing.

Gene wandered out of the shower and into an empty room. For a second his heart stopped.

He started to walk out into the corridor and stopped. He was naked. And he was a guest in someone else's house. He roughly towelled himself off and yanked on his jeans. The water was still running down his chest as he walked to the door and started to towel-dry his hair. 'Rory?'

The corridor was empty.

His heart rate quickened. He opened his mouth to shout again and then he stopped. And listened.

He could hear murmuring voices. There was only one other person in this house apart from Rory. Cordelia.

His curiosity was piqued. He took a few steps towards the door to Cordelia's room. It was ajar and he could see Rory sitting up on the bed next to Cordelia, drinking a glass of milk.

He put his hand on the door to push through and apologise but the words stopped him dead.

'My mom's up there.'

Gene winced as his stomach clenched.

The one thing he couldn't control. Just how much his son missed his mother.

It was normal. It was natural. Rory had attended a few nurseries and seen lots of other kids being picked up by their mommies. Gene always kept a photograph of Mindy around. He told Rory that was his mom and that she'd loved him very much.

Rory asked questions sometimes, but not often. Maybe he hadn't spoken about Mindy enough? The trouble was, there was no one else to tell Rory about Mindy, and what Gene knew wasn't really that much. He wasn't really into embellishments. But that looked like the only solution he had left.

His son had just told a perfect stranger that he wanted to be an astronaut because his mom was up in the stars. It was a story that families the world over told little kids. That someone they missed or loved who had died was up in the stars, watching over them.

Rory had long held a fascination with the planets and stars. But he'd never mentioned his mother. Gene had no idea that was the way he'd been thinking.

He was frozen. His feet rooted to the floor. But the woman who'd been prickly at their first meeting seemed to be managing around Rory.

In normal circumstances he would walk in

and take over. But was that really best for Rory right now?

Rory had just told Cordelia Greenway something he hadn't shared with his dad. That made Gene's skin prickle. Was he failing his child? Wasn't he being the best dad that he could be?

His mouth felt dry.

He kept listening, watching through the gap in the door.

It felt like prowling. And he certainly wasn't doing that. Rory was safe.

And right now he was seeing a side of Cordelia he hadn't noticed before.

He could see she was dedicated to her work. The staff at the institute appeared to both like and respect her.

It almost made him want to push what had happened the other day out of his head. But he couldn't. It sat there, churning away in his mind, making him wonder what he was missing.

He could hear Cordelia still talking softly to Rory. Occasionally there was a little tremor in her voice. But she also sounded reassuring.

He closed his eyes for a second. Could he

imagine Karen ever doing something like this? The truth was, no. He'd been hurt when she'd walked away. She'd been clear that she couldn't see herself taking on someone else's child. And that had hurt. Because Rory had been like a bolt out of the blue to him too. But he couldn't walk away. He would never have dreamed of it.

But here was sometimes prickly Cordelia being sweet to his son in a way he would never have expected.

When Rory asked about getting a new mommy and if she would love him, Gene's stomach clenched so hard it felt like it was made of lead.

Cordelia's answer seemed so simple. And completely and utterly true. He would never be with someone who couldn't love his son as much as he did. They were a package deal.

His heart squeezed in his chest. The woman he'd been angry with a few days ago got that. She had got that about him straight away. And as he watched she settled Rory under her arm and started reading him his favourite story book.

Now his heart gave an unsteady flutter. Rory

looked so comfortable there. His little body had adopted the slumped position it normally did just before he fell asleep. Sure enough, like clockwork, only a few pages into the book Rory's eyelids started to droop.

Gene took a deep breath and collected himself, willing that he'd look as if he'd just appeared this second.

He stuck his head around the door and whispered, 'Cordelia?'

She looked up and stopped reading. Her eyes widened as he realised he still hadn't put a shirt on.

He almost hesitated, then dismissed it. She was a doctor, she'd seen more than enough naked torsos in her line of work. He walked over to the bed. 'Apologies,' he whispered. 'I was in the shower. Rory hasn't really grasped the concept of patience.'

She looked down at the mop of blond hair and ruffled it with her fingers. His head was completely sagging now. He was fast asleep.

'I'm not too good at the whole patience thing myself.' She looked up and met his gaze. The sincerity in her green eyes made him catch his breath.

'I'm sorry. I was in the shower,' he repeated. Crazy. He'd already said that. What was wrong with him?

'So I can see.' A smile danced across her lips as her eyes fixed on his bare chest.

He held out his hands and smiled back. 'What can I say? I didn't have time to put all my clothes on. I came out of the shower and realised I was missing a child.'

She shook her head. 'Poor excuse. You never got paged when you were in the shower when you were working as a resident?'

The hours and workload of resident doctors were notorious. By the time every doctor had finished training they had dozens of stories to tell.

She tutted and shook her head. 'I can't believe you don't know how to do the ten-second soaked-to-fully-clothed dance.'

There was a gleam in her eyes. She was teasing. Of course she was.

He shook his head and slid his arms under Rory's body. 'I can assure you I'm a professional.' He winked. 'I can do it in eight. Give me a sec, let me put Rory to bed.'

He kissed Rory on top of his head and walked back through to their room, putting him into the double bed and pulling the cover over him. He grabbed a grey T-shirt and tugged it over his head. She was standing at the door with her arms folded over her chest. She tilted her head to the side. 'If you can do it in eight, then how come you didn't manage?'

He stepped closer. He hadn't even realised she was wearing a pair of cute pink pyjamas. Now she was standing up, even though every part of her was covered, he could see the way the jersey hugged her curves.

He gave a shake of his head and held up his hands as he kept his voice low. 'Clothes aren't really required when you're missing a four-year-old.' He rubbed his hands on his jeans. 'Just be glad I put on these.'

She started to laugh then put her hand up to her mouth and stepped back. 'Sorry, don't want to wake Rory.'

'Oh, don't worry. You won't wake Rory. Once

he goes to sleep, that's it. Nothing—not even a freight train—could wake him.'

She smiled again. 'Sleep's a funny thing. I could sleep within a few seconds when I was resident, but I was always on alert, waiting for the next page. But as soon as I got home? That's it. I was out like a light—just like Rory. I once slept through guys drilling on the road outside.'

Gene felt something wash over him. Completely unexpected.

'I used to do that.' The words came out almost on autopilot.

She met his gaze. 'And you don't any more?'

He glanced at the sleeping figure on the bed. Rory's head was resting on the pillow and he was curled into a ball. When Gene sucked in a breath he almost juddered. 'I haven't slept like that since Rory arrived.'

She blinked. And for a second he thought he'd made her feel uncomfortable. But she just gave a gentle shake of her head. 'I can't imagine how it must be to hear out of the blue that you've got a child. And that his mom was so sick. But whatever you've done over the last few years, it's worked. He's a gorgeous kid. Bright, articulate, intelligent and…' she smiled '…very, very sweet.'

For a second he thought there was a flash of sadness across her face. But as quickly as it had appeared, it vanished again.

She pulled up one of legs behind her, catching her foot by the ankle and letting it click loudly. 'Sorry, aches and pains. I get that way sometimes. Must be my old dance injuries— or my age.'

He put his hand at the back of his neck. 'Mine too. But it's an old football injury.'

She gave a smile. 'Well, I can't claim any kind of sport injuries. My biggest sport these days is how quickly I can read a book.'

He didn't quite believe her. She was only wearing thin pyjamas and although she had a few curves, there was no hint of heaviness in her frame.

'Did you recognise that book that Rory made you read? You seemed to relate easily.'

She laughed. 'It's a book. I always relate to books. When I was a kid you were only allowed four books with your library card. I tried to pretend to be another kid and get an extra card so I could check out eight books at a time.'

'Did your plan work?'

'Are you joking? My disguise was very flawed. I only took my outdoor jacket off.'

He couldn't help but laugh out loud too. He was watching the easy, casual way Cordelia was chatting—as if it were completely normal to be chatting to someone she didn't know that well in her pyjamas.

But that was the life of a doctor. Running around in scrubs permanently wasn't that different from pjs.

She reached over and touched his arm. It was just her thumb that came into contact with his still-damp skin, but he could almost hear a hiss. Even in the dim light her bright green eyes seemed to draw him in.

Female contact. When was the last time he'd had some?

He didn't even want to think about that. And certainly not now. In a semi-dark room with a woman with chestnut-brown curls resting on her shoulders.

'I think I'm going to go downstairs and make some toast. Want some?'

He could sense it. That tiny hint of breaking the ice between them again. Things had been awkward these last few days and he had to admit he didn't like it. This was the first time they'd been face to face again. And the dim lights and thin layers of clothes made things seem much more…intimate.

He glanced back at Rory, whose little chest was rising and falling deeply. He was sound asleep.

It must only be around nine o'clock. He couldn't pretend to be tired so he nodded and followed her down the staircase to the kitchen.

Cordelia moved with ease, putting on the kettle and popping wholemeal bread into the toaster.

'What can I do?'

She waved her hand. 'Sit down. It's only toast. What do you want? Low-fat spread, butter, jam or marmalade?'

He leaned back and met her gaze. He wanted to talk. He wanted to talk so badly it almost made his stomach ache. He wanted to ask her about Rory, what she thought about what he'd said, if it meant that Rory was disappointed in him, if he just wasn't enough on his own?

But he couldn't do that. Cordelia might be nice. She might be a fellow doctor. She might be dedicated to her work and respected by her patients. And she might have been good with Rory. She might also be extremely attractive—a fact he was trying very hard to ignore.

But he couldn't forget his instincts. There was something he just couldn't quite put his finger on.

Cordelia Greenway was keeping secrets.

It was there. In every sideways glance. Every careful answer.

The toast popped and he realised he hadn't answered her question. He jumped up and walked over to the fridge, pulling out what he needed. 'I love the way you guys call it jam when it's really jelly.'

She wrinkled her nose. 'No way. Jelly is the stuff that wobbles—that you have with ice cream.' She raised her eyebrows. 'And I've seen how much Rory loves ice cream.'

She buttered the toast quickly as the kettle boiled and she set down the mugs. He still couldn't stop smiling at the thought of Rory with the ice cream.

She sighed as she sat opposite him and leaned her head on one hand. It was the first time he'd noticed how tired she looked. Of course. Not only did she have two unexpected house guests, she also had the whole responsibility of the institute on her shoulders. It must be tough.

'So,' she started, 'how do you feel things are with your part of the trials?'

He'd been holding his breath, wondering if she'd mention what had happened between them a few days ago. And he looked at her steadily, sure that his eyes were asking the question that wouldn't quite form on his lips.

There was something in her return gaze. A determination and stubbornness that he expected had been there for a long time.

He licked his lips and tried not to smile. They weren't going to talk about it. Even though they had complete privacy.

Fine. He could do this. He could play this game.

'I think the trial is going well. Apart from

what happened with Aryssa.' He had to say it—her exclusion would be detrimental to the trial. 'From a review of the case notes and blood-work it looks as if around sixty-five per cent of the trial candidates are showing clear signs of improvement. That's really impressive for a trial.' He gave a wry smile. 'Of course, things are complicated by the range of comorbidities suffered by the patients. But that's what makes them real. And that's what makes these studies more worthwhile than others.'

Cordelia gave a slow nod. 'Sometimes I love the studies—sometimes I hate them. I get lost in the zebrafish studies. They're such remarkable creatures. If only our hearts could regenerate the same way. Then we'd have no heart failure, no tired and worn-out cells.' She gave a sad kind of smile. 'Maybe a chance to create better pathways for some.'

It was cardiac-speak. Only a fellow cardiac specialist would understand it. But it struck a little chord in him.

She was drumming her fingers on the table but looked up and met his gaze. 'It sounds like your study is doing better than mine.' She hesitated for a second then reached over and squeezed his hand. It was an unexpected move that took him by surprise.

That was a few times now. A few times when her skin had just brushed against his and...

'I'm glad. I'm glad for you, glad for Rory, and for all the other patients who might get to lead an easier life.'

He could see it. The shine in her eyes. The truth. The sincerity. And it was confusing him. That, and the tingles shooting up his arm. He couldn't quite get a handle on what was happening.

She pulled her hand back and wrapped both of them around her mug of tea. 'The research can be hard. Some find it soul-destroying because there are no fast answers, no magic cures out there. But it never gets old. So I try to remember that every day is a new day, with a world of possibilities.'

Her voice was quiet, soft with a distinct edge of hope.

'That's your thing,' he said quickly.

'My what?' She frowned.

He couldn't help but smile. 'I asked you the

other day what your "thing" was. You said you didn't know.'

She was still frowning and looked totally confused. She shook her head. 'But we didn't do that weird fist bump thing.'

His smile widened. 'No, that's my thing. Mine and Rory's. But that's twice now I've heard you say it. *It never gets old. Every day is a new day with a world of possibilities.*' He lifted his hands and shrugged his shoulders. 'There. It's official. It's your thing.'

She tilted her head to one side and looked thoughtful. 'I didn't think I had a thing.'

He lifted his mug towards hers. 'Well, you do. To things.'

She laughed as she chinked her mug against his. 'Okay, then, to things.' She glanced over her shoulder. 'How about some more toast?'

CHAPTER FIVE

'HOW ABOUT A bit of fun?'

She turned sideways. Was he talking to her or to Rory? The other night had been a weird mixture of feeling the most relaxed she'd been since Gene and Rory had arrived, and a crazy spin cycle of other emotions. One minute she was thinking about the relationship Gene had with his son—how it made her ache inside and gave her strange pangs of envy. The next minute she was trying to fight the crazy, stupid waves of attraction she was feeling to the handsome Texan.

It was ridiculous. He was a short-term colleague—albeit a very handsome one. And there wasn't the slightest chance he was attracted to her.

Except…

That sometimes she caught a look, a sideways glance that made her heart trip over itself. Or there was the fleeting tingle when their skins connected and her senses flipped into over-drive. Maybe she was going crazy. Maybe she was finally losing her mind, because she never did this. Never.

Something washed over her. She'd never even had these crazy mixed-up feelings about Han—and he'd been in her life for a few years, not a few weeks. She couldn't deny that when he'd left she'd been shattered and hurt. But was that all really over Han, or had it been about the gradual sinking in of the news from her con-sultant that she shouldn't have kids?

The truth was she hadn't really given her-self time to think about it all. It had been much easier just to immerse herself in work up until now...

She wasn't the kind of girl to fall head over heels for some totally unsuitable guy. She'd al-ways been far too practical for that. Why should it change now?

But for the last few days things had been much more relaxed around the workplace and at home, and she liked that.

She'd liked the vibe and warmth that seemed to emanate both from Rory and Gene.

'Cordelia?' The voice broke into her thoughts. 'How about a bit of fun?'

Gene was standing at the kitchen doorway, leaning against the jamb with his arms folded.

There was something about the look on his face. Had he been reading her thoughts? Fun with the Texan cowboy?

Her heartbeat gave a little flutter and she ducked her head as heat rushed into her cheeks. She pushed the ridiculous thoughts from her head as she turned to face him. 'What do you mean?'

There was something about this guy. He just had to give her *that* look. The one where his eyes twinkled and she wanted to dig underneath and see what mischief he was hiding. It was so easy to be pulled in.

He raised his eyebrows and held out his hands. 'Apparently, we're in Geneva. One of the most beautiful cities in the world. I haven't had a chance to see any of it. And I've no idea what's suitable for kids.' He stepped towards her. 'You don't need to work today—I've checked. How about you show us around a little?'

His chocolate-brown eyes fixed on hers. A little shiver ran down her spine. He'd checked her schedule. He'd made sure she was free. It could just be that he wanted someone to show him around—someone who was familiar with the territory. But the butterflies in her stomach were hoping it was something else entirely.

How stupid was that? He was a colleague. He was here on a temporary basis. She wasn't in a position to think about anything else. So why was she?

But something inside gave her a little push. The words were out before her brain had any more time to think about it. 'Sure, why not?'

Geneva. The most gorgeous city in the world. Of course he'd want to see it. When she'd first got here she'd been in awe of its beauty—from the Alps to the lakes. But where to take a kid?

There was so much to see in the city. A museum of natural history. The cathedral, and the Jardin Botanique. But Rory was too young for most of that yet.

She wrinkled her nose for a second as she

scanned her brain, stopping at the biggest thing she could think of. 'Do you trust me to find something that a kid will like?'

Gene tipped his head to the side and looked thoughtful for a second. 'Isn't everyone really a kid at heart?'

There was something about the way he said it. As if it was the most natural thing in the world. She felt a little tug inside her. And she knew exactly where to take them. She picked up the phone to call a taxi.

'Get your jackets.' She smiled. 'And be prepared to get wet.'

They headed towards the city. Rory was excited already. He was chatting as he was sandwiched between them in the taxi. Gene hadn't heard the instructions Cordelia had given the driver, and he'd expected the driver to head towards the city centre, but instead he circled the outside and took them in another direction. After twenty minutes he realised they were skirting the edges of Lake Geneva.

'We're going to the lake?' he asked.

Cordelia nodded as the taxi pulled up to drop

them off. 'What do all kids love? Water. Just wait until Rory sees just how many boats there are here.'

As the sun was warm, Gene carried their jackets as they walked to the lake shore. Rory let out a little gasp at the wide expanse of Lake Geneva. He turned to Gene with big eyes. 'Daddy, is this all ours? Do we get to play here?'

Gene laughed out loud. He reached down and grasped the little hand, bending towards the excited face. 'Yeah, but we have to share it with other people.'

'Come over here.' Cordelia was standing next to a telescope that looked out over the lake. She slid some coins into the slot as he held Rory up to the foot stand. 'Just how big is this place?' Gene asked.

She waved out her hand. 'It's forty-five miles long—the largest body of water in Switzerland, crescent-shaped and is shared between Switzerland and France.'

She gave a little smile as she looked over her shoulder. 'And it has the distinct advantage of being surrounded by mountains.'

He looked over at the snow-topped Alps behind the body of water. It really was one of the most picturesque places he'd ever seen.

He gave a nod. 'I'll give you a ten for the view.' His eyes ran up and down her body. He didn't mean to. It just happened. Cordelia was wearing well-fitting jeans and a long-sleeved red top. Her hair was tied back off her face, but the brisk breeze from the lake still made stray strands whip around her face.

She leaned down next to Rory and pointed out all the types of craft on the lake. It was littered with mainly white boats—pleasure cruisers, luxury yachts, a rescue craft, even an old replica paddle steamer. She pointed to some smaller yellow vessels. 'These are *mouettes*. They'll take us across to the other side of the lake. There's something special over there.'

'Can we, Daddy? Can we go?' Rory was jumping up and down at the thought of getting on one of the small ferries.

Gene could see them crossing the lake in a regular manner. They were obviously well used. 'Sure, why not?'

Cordelia led them to a boarding station and they climbed aboard one of the *mouettes*. The boats were covered and sat low in the water. They picked a seat near the front. Within a few seconds Rory was laughing as the air rushed in his face as they crossed the lake.

Cordelia sat in the seat next to him, her arm casually resting on Rory's shoulders as she pointed out other things as they crossed the lake. Ten minutes later they reached the other side.

'This is the west bank,' she said as they climbed out. 'There's lots to do here. But the first thing is this.' She grinned as she pointed straight ahead. 'Jet d'Eau is the world's tallest water fountain.'

Gene frowned as he looked towards the stone jetty. Was this some kind of trick? 'What are we looking at?'

She grinned as she glanced at her watch and she grabbed Rory's hand and stuck one finger in the air. 'Let me check the wind direction. We could get drenched any second.'

Gene had no idea what she was talking about. Something flickered in his brain. Something about a soccer championship. There was a rumble underneath them. Like a train passing beneath their feet. People had gathered around, everyone glancing at their watches. Rory was bouncing. He could feel the excitement in the air.

Seconds later it happened. A huge rushing noise, and water seemed to explode out of the lake, shooting more than a hundred feet into the air.

The effect was instantaneous. Everyone surrounding the area jumped back automatically—even though they were far back from the jet of water.

Tiny droplets started to shower down around them. Gene held out his hands in wonder. 'What on earth is it?' he said above the roar of water.

Cordelia was grinning, her eyes firmly fixed on Rory. 'I told you. It's Jet d'Eau. The largest water fountain in Switzerland.' Her eyes were gleaming.

'And what? They just switch it on?'

She nodded. 'It's been here for more than a hundred and thirty years. It was further along at first—originally as a safety valve for the hydraulic power network—but they realised how much people loved it, and they moved it to here.'

She held out her hands and pointed to the stream of water. 'We have to be careful. If the wind changes we could be drenched in seconds.'

Gene was shaking his head in wonder at the sight. People were crowded around, attracted by the sudden gush of water. He laughed at Cordelia as she grabbed Rory's hand to stamp in the puddles that had appeared around their feet. 'Five hundred litres of water a second,' she shouted over her shoulder to Gene, 'at about a hundred and twenty miles an hour.'

'Isn't it great, Daddy?' yelled Rory as his baseball boots started to get darker and darker with the water.

Gene swept him up under his arm. 'Hey, buddy. Do you want to have wet feet all day?'

He looked down at Cordelia's equally damp red baseball boots. 'I did warn you.' She grinned. She shook her hair and showered him in tiny droplets of water. 'Come on, we'll head into the left bank. It's fun.'

She led them through the picturesque medieval streets towards a beautiful garden. It was full of families and street performers, and she took Rory by the hand towards the middle of the park where a large feature clock made of brightly coloured flowers was situated.

'It's huge,' breathed Rory. 'Does it work?'

Cordelia nodded. 'The hands move. And the flowers change colour depending on the season. So, it's red, pink and orange now. In a few months it could be yellow and purple.'

Cordelia chatted easily, guiding Rory next to a mini train station, which, of course, he loved. The train was old-fashioned, bright red and they climbed aboard easily. She leaned over next to Gene and whispered in his ear, 'This takes around thirty minutes. It goes along the edge of the lake and takes us to another park.'

He slung his arm around Rory's shoulder and relaxed into the ride. For someone who'd seemed a little uncomfortable around kids, Cordelia seemed to have warmed up. She chatted to Rory as the PA system on the train pointed out the UN buildings on the other side of the lake and all the other tourist attractions. Her scent drifted over towards him as she kept bending down to talk to Rory. He couldn't help but keep watching her. Her skin was bright and clear, her eyes sparkling, and there was only a hint of lipstick on her lips. He almost didn't notice as the train pulled up next to a sandy beach with a massive play park.

'Want to get off?' asked Cordelia 'This is the baby *plage*—the children's beach. There's loads here for kids to do.'

Gene looked around. The beach and surrounding area was already full of families and kids and looked perfect. The kids' area was equipped with a lawn, a sandy area and an unusual set of climbing equipment under a shady tree. Rory was buzzing instantly.

'I want to try that!' he said, pointing at the equipment.

Gene nodded and climbed out of the train, holding out his hand for them both to follow. There were swings, climbing frames, and a mini rope bridge between two big tree branches, all in a safe, secluded area where children could easily be supervised. Water buoys marked the shallow area of the lake where kids could paddle safely. Cordelia and Gene sat on the beach together while Rory had a ball, instantly making friends with the international array of kids around him.

Gene leaned back on his hands as Cordelia's eyes flitted from one kid to the next. 'Isn't it interesting?'

'What?'

'The language of kids. They're all chattering away to each other in different languages. But it's almost like they understand each other.'

'If only adults could do the same,' said Cordelia wistfully.

He turned to her and smiled. 'We get so caught up in languages. I only speak two. But sometimes I feel as if I really need to speak them all.'

Something flicked into his head. 'The Japanese investors. You're meeting them on Tuesday, aren't you?'

She nodded and brushed some hair from her face. 'They pushed their visit back so I've had some more time to prepare.'

'How are you feeling about it? Are you okay with that?'

There was only a flicker of hesitation. 'Yes, I've met a few of the investors before. Franc always shows them around the entire institute and invites them to talk to staff—even patients if they want to.'

He paused for a second, not wanting to step on her toes. 'But you've never had to meet them on your own before?'

She bit her bottom lip and shook her head, pulling her knees up to her chest. 'Nope.'

There were no further words—and that told Gene all he needed to know. 'If you want, I can make sure I'm around—to answer any questions they might have on the cardiomyopathy study.'

He didn't want her to think he was trying to push his way in. Cordelia would know more about the institute than he could ever hope to. But before he'd even contemplated taking the job here, he'd pored over their research study. He was confident he could cover any questions they might have, and wanted to take the pressure off her a little if he could.

She gave a thoughtful nod. Her eyes were still fixed on Rory on the climbing frame. 'That would be great, thanks. Another person to answer questions on the studies would be great. I know the zebrafish stuff back to front. The cardiomyopathy study—I've never taken the lead on that. I'd like it if you were available.'

Her head rested on her knees and she looked sideways at him. The shade from the trees cast a shadow over her face but still let him focus on her bright green eyes framed with thick dark lashes. She had virtually no make-up on today. Her cheeks were tinged pink from the fresh breeze from the lake. The breeze carried her scent over the short distance between them again, something tinged with a hint of rose and orange.

Just the smell and the intensity of her gaze sent a little pulse rushing through him. His brain was taking in the words 'I'd like it if you were available' to a whole other place. He spoke quickly, to try and stop his thoughts going any-place else. 'Anything to help out. After all, we are invading your home.'

His voice was quiet and she lifted her head and leaned forward a little. It was odd how glad he felt about that. How he liked the fact he could see a freckle at the base of her neck, or the way a strand of hair was coiled around her ear.

She gave a soft smile. 'You're not invad-ing my home. It's Franc's. In fact, we're both home invaders.' She closed her eyes and let out a breath. 'I'll need to talk to the insurance company again. Things seem to have ground to a complete halt.'

'Daddy, Daddy.' Rory ran over, his cheeks flushed. 'Can I have some juice?'

He was breathing heavily, his eyes bright with excitement. Before Gene had a chance to speak Cordelia pushed herself up and dusted off her jeans. 'I have an idea. How about ice cream? There's an ice-cream cart just a little further along, next to an old-fashioned merry-go-round. Why don't we head in that direction?'

Rory jumped up and down. 'Ice cream, yeah!'

Gene smiled and glanced at his watch. 'Sure, why not.' Cordelia held out her hand towards Rory and he eagerly slid his little hand into hers.

The walk was a pleasant stroll around the edge of the lake. The old quarter surrounding them was quaint, with winding streets filled with unusual and quirky shops. The vintage merry-go-round had a little crowd around it and Rory laughed as he clambered on the biggest blue horse he could find, bobbing up and down merrily as the ride slowly went around.

Cordelia waved every time Rory passed and

Gene got out his phone to snap some pictures. Rory was having a great day. His cheeks glowed and eyes sparkled. He gave a shout whenever he circled around again and Gene felt his heart swell with pride. 'Daddy! Delia!' Rory shouted.

Gene laughed at the shortened version of Cordelia's name. Her cheeks flushed as she laughed too. 'Only my old nana used to call me Delia. I haven't been called that in years.'

The merry-go-round started to slow and Gene reached forward to grab Rory. He swung him up onto his hip. 'What kind of ice cream would you like?' he asked his son.

'Chocolate!' shouted Rory.

'Chocolate it is.' Gene smiled as they walked over to the ice-cream cart.

Five minutes later they walked in the sunshine along the edge of the lake. The sun was bright and the ice cream quickly ran down their arms.

He'd asked Cordelia this morning on a spur-of-the-moment thought. It had seemed wrong to explore the city without her when he knew she was free. But even though he was curious about her, he'd never expected to enjoy himself quite so much.

Cordelia was definitely an attractive woman, but the more time he spent in her company, the more he found herself attracted to her.

They'd been here two and a half weeks. His contract was only for a month. This was a bad idea. He knew that. So why wasn't his brain listening?

Rory was still hyper. And he was a pleasure to be around. By the time they wandered through the old quarter streets and looked in the windows of all the quaint shops, he finally started to tire. Time had marched on and Rory was up in Gene's arms, snuggled into his shoulders.

Gene smiled as he adjusted Rory's position. 'He's not quite as light as he looks. How do you feel about grabbing an early dinner?'

Cordelia nodded. The day had been so nice. She really didn't want it to end. She looked around. 'Sure, why not? Do you have a preference where we go?'

He shook his head. 'Just somewhere that I can put Rory down on a seat.'

They walked a little further through the streets until they came to a friendly-looking German restaurant. A woman was trying to usher tourists in from the streets. She waved them over when she glanced at Rory. *'Anglais? Français?'*

Cordelia smiled. *'Anglais.'*

'Come, come.' The woman gestured. 'I find you somewhere for little one.'

Gene grinned and raised his eyebrows at Cordelia. 'What do you think?'

She shrugged and nodded. 'Why not?'

The woman's smile was broad as she showed them into a booth with leather seats on either side. Gene hesitated for a second. 'Do you mind if I put Rory down on one side and let him lie flat?'

'Of course not.'

Rory didn't even make a sound as his father laid him down—obviously the excitement of the day had all been too much for him.

Within minutes they had menus and drinks—a beer for Gene and a glass of wine for Cordelia. The restaurant was informal and friendly. Their waitress gave them her recommendation from the menu: *sauerbraten* over *spaetzle*—a marinated pot roast served with a buttery *spaetzle* pasta and spicy red cabbage—and they were soon eating heartily.

'So, what do you do normally on a day off? Have we ruined things for you?'

Something inside her gave a little buzz at his interest in her. 'Of course not. I've had a great day.'

She leaned towards his ear and whispered, 'I'll let you into a secret. I've always secretly wanted to go on that merry-go-round.'

'You should have said something. You could have gone on with Rory—he would have loved that.'

She laughed. 'And how would I have looked—a thirty-something woman sitting alongside all the kids?'

He raised his glass of beer towards her. 'I think you would have looked good.'

It was the expression in his eyes as he said it. The little flirtatious glimmer. Or was she imagining it? There had been several times today that their gazes had meshed and she'd felt... something. A connection.

A connection she kept wondering if she really was experiencing.

Because, if she was, it was completely messing with her brain.

Gene's long legs were stretched out beneath the table alongside hers. His head was facing her, leaning on one hand. The fingers of his other hand stroked the outside of his beer glass.

Her thoughts immediately went elsewhere, making her skin tingle. What on earth was wrong with her?

She picked up her wineglass and took a gulp. There was an amused expression on his face as he watched her through heavy lids.

'What?' she asked as she glanced over her shoulder. 'What is it?'

He gave a small shrug. 'I don't know. Every now and then, just out of nowhere, it's like you have a flash of panic.'

She knew exactly what he was talking about. She was feeling the flash of panic right now—all entirely related to him.

'No, I don't.' She tried to sound casual.

He straightened a little, still looking amused. 'Yeah. You do. I can see it in your eyes. I can always tell when you're about to change the subject or walk away.'

She bit her bottom lip for a second and tried to stop the instant throw-away remarks that circled in her head.

She looked down at those long legs again. Nope. Not helping.

She stared back at those brown eyes. Darn it. Why did they have to look so deep? Like something you just swirl around and get lost in?

'Well, I haven't walked away now. Or changed the subject, have I?'

His shoulder brushed against hers. 'No, you haven't.' He looked over at Rory. 'But now we're away from work, and little ears are sleeping, how about we have some adult chat?'

Heat rushed into her cheeks like some kind of race car zooming around a track as she shifted on the bench seat. 'What do you mean?'

He still had that darned sexy smile on his lips. He gave another shrug. 'I mean, let's talk. I share a house with you but I feel as if I don't really know much about you.'

'You know that jelly is jam, I like chocolate, and red baseball boots are my favourite footwear.'

He tapped his fingers on the table with a determined glint in his eyes. He wasn't going to be put off. 'Okay, then. I've told you about Rory's mom. Do you have a secret husband or boyfriend stashed away somewhere?'

She shook her head. 'Nope. Not right now. I've had a few boyfriends. But nothing lasted more than a year.' She gave a laugh. 'I'm not deliberately antisocial but I guess for the last while I've just been so focused on my work.'

'That's understandable. Okay, so I know about this work—at the institute. But where did you work before?'

'I trained in London, then worked in cardiology. I worked at the Royal Brompton and King's College.'

He gave an appreciative look. 'But you decided to have a change?'

She'd answered questions before about her career change. And she didn't like telling lies. But she wasn't quite sure she was ready to share about her condition—particularly when he'd been annoyed with her a few days ago. They were back to a place that she liked. She didn't want to do anything to spoil that. 'Yeah, I decided I wanted to work in research. I loved clinical care, but I've always had big-picture thoughts. About where I can do the best work, to help the most people.'

She was almost holding her breath—hoping it sounded plausible.

Gene glanced over at Rory. 'I feel like that about this work. My brain knows the processes of research…' he gave a rueful smile '…but the inner me is impatient. I wish I had a magic wand and could just know everything now. I sometimes want to jump a hundred years into the future so I don't need to wait to find out what improvements we can make, and what difference all the research does.'

She swallowed the lump in her throat. She understood, but she didn't feel quite ready to share why. 'But you have a really good reason to think like that.' She was glancing at the mop of blond curls at the other side of the table. 'If Rory were mine, I'd think like that too.'

She turned to face him. 'You want to make the difference now. For Rory. For the patients.' Her voice dropped a little. 'For people like Mindy.'

He ran his fingers through his hair. 'I think about that a lot. If Mindy's condition hadn't been so severe she would still be here. Rory would still have his mom.' He looked off into the distance and his voice cracked a little. 'Maybe I wouldn't even have met my son.'

He put his hands back on the table and she could see the tiny shake. That was all it took. She gently rested her hand over his and gave it a little squeeze.

He turned to her with pain in his eyes. 'What if things had been different?'

There was a whole world of possibilities there. If Mindy had lived. If Rory hadn't been affected by the gene. If only...

His other hand reached over and stroked along her arm. It was clear it was an automatic response for him, his mind looked a million miles away.

Her heart was thudding in her chest nearly as loudly as the sound in her ears. Her skin was on fire. It was almost as if her insides were twisting around. She knew she had to ask a question, even if it wasn't the right thing to do.

'What would you have done—if you'd known Mindy was pregnant?'

She could almost see the tiny hairs on his

arms stand on end. A pained expression crossed his face. He shook his head and ran his fingers through his hair. 'How can I answer that? It's impossible.' He shook his head again. 'And how do I answer—as a parent or a physician?'

'You're both, Gene. Answer as you.'

His lips pressed together tightly and he put his hand on his heart. 'No. I can't. I just can't. Maybe if you'd asked me before...maybe if I'd known Mindy had hypertrophic cardiomyopathy. Would I really have asked a woman I'd only known briefly to put her life at risk to have my child?'

She could see the pain on his face. A deep frown creased his forehead. 'What kind of egotistical maniac would I be to do that?'

She understood. She understood what he was saying. As a physician, if he was presented with a patient with Mindy's condition who was newly pregnant, he would have to consider a very serious conversation with her.

He let out a long sigh. 'Everything's different now. Rory is real. He's here. He's not a maybe. He's just my whole life. I can't imagine for a second not being his father.' He closed his eyes for a second. 'I'd met someone. By the time I found out about Rory I was actually living with someone.'

Something rushed through her. 'Who?'

He shrugged. 'Karen. She was...nice. But when she found out about Rory...' He shook his head. 'And that was before she even knew that he had the heart condition.'

'She left?' It was odd. Tears sprang to her eyes. He'd had someone who'd left. Just like she'd had. She and Gene were more similar than she'd ever admit to.

Gene nodded. 'Yeah, she left.' He gave a wry smile. 'I can't admit it didn't sting. But do I really blame her? We'd only known each other less than a year, and all of a sudden an unknown kid appeared out of nowhere. It wasn't fair. I know that. But at the time it didn't just feel like a rejection of me. It felt like a rejection of the kid I didn't even know yet.'

Cordelia nodded slowly. She was still watching Rory. The odd little flare of jealousy she'd felt there had quickly subsided and she was struggling to understand it. But she could understand the rest. The feeling of rejection. The hurt.

She shook her head too. 'But look what you've got, Gene. Isn't he worth a million broken hearts?'

Gene caught her eye and smiled. It made her catch her breath. A connection. An understanding. 'You're right. I put Karen behind me a long time ago. I had too much to think about. Too much to learn and too much to do.' He sighed. 'I'm still on that learning curve every day.'

She smiled again. 'Doesn't every parent feel the same?'

He gave a thoughtful nod. 'I guess they do. But, then, there's the rest of it. His condition. His future.' There was the tiniest crack in his voice. 'And I struggle enough trying to think about the things I can't control with his condition.' He took a deep breath and met her gaze. 'So the sad truth about me is that now, if you asked me if I would have told Mindy to put her own health first, the honest and selfish answer is, no. I wouldn't. Because I wouldn't want to miss out on the joy that is my son.'

She could feel herself holding her breath as he continued to speak.

He looked away from her. 'Does that make

me a bad person? Does that make me a bad doctor? Because it feels like it does. I guess the real answer is that I'm glad I didn't have to find out. Rory is the light of my life. I can't imagine what life would be like if he wasn't in it. The fact that I know he will have the same condition as his mom makes me appreciate every second that I have. It makes me work harder because I know that I could lose him—and that terrifies me more than anything. If only life could be simpler. If only there could be a magic cure.' He sighed. 'If only our genes didn't define us.'

A chill swept through her body. She understood better than he would ever know. Maybe she should tell him? But then what? That would be like revealing a part of herself she wasn't quite ready to share. She'd only known them a few weeks. She didn't want his pity or his sympathy—even though she understood his feelings of rejection. The responsible part of her felt that, as a fellow medic, she should tell him, just in case she should ever feel ill at work again. But the emotional part of her just couldn't do that. She didn't want him to think of her as a patient.

Her brain spun around. How did she want him to think of her?

She was so confused right now. As for how she felt about Rory?

He was the best kid she'd ever met. She reached over and grabbed Gene's hand.

'I know you don't think it, but I understand better than you can imagine. Rory is fabulous and you're a brilliant father. Don't doubt that for second. You've done a brilliant job. Anyone can see that.'

His chocolate-brown eyes met hers. Their gazes meshed. She didn't want to look away— not for a second. The world was moving around about them, but right now she could swear they were the only two people on the planet. If only she could capture this moment in time. Her heart squeezed in her chest.

The way he was looking at her made her skin tingle. It made her heart miss a beat. The corners of his lips edged upwards. His voice was a husky whisper. 'I'm glad we met, Cordelia Greenway.'

He leaned forward and pressed his forehead against hers. She could feel his warm breath dancing across her skin. Smell the hint of beer on his breath, mixed with the tang of aftershave.

His fingers intertwined with hers.

And he left them there.

So much was spinning through her head right now.

But she said the thing that was in her heart. 'I'm glad we met too, Gene Du Bois.'

He had no idea. No idea how much that made her insides twist around.

With hope.

With regret.

With affection.

And with the wish he was staying a whole lot longer.

CHAPTER SIX

GENE LOOKED AT the results in front of him. His heart sank into his shoes. No. Please, no.

A new collection of patients were being screened for their suitability to take part in the next trial. He'd met all of them over the last few days, all at varying stages of disease with their cardiomyopathy. All patients required extensive workouts, medical history and a whole array of tests before they could be accepted on the trials.

Lea Keller was a Swiss national in her twenties. She'd been lucky. She'd played professional sports and her condition had been picked up in her teenage years.

But staring at the test results meant that Gene was going to have the difficult conversation he'd spoken with Cordelia about just the other day.

He gestured to Marie. 'Can you call Lea Keller in, please?'

Marie took only a few seconds to pick up on

the expression on his face. 'No problem, Dr Du Bois. I'll get her straight away.'

Lea appeared in his office a few minutes later. She gave Gene a wide smile. Cardiac patients were generally very smart. 'Don't tell me, I'm anaemic again?'

Gene kept his face impassive. Anaemia would be easy to deal with—this was not.

'Take a seat.' He gestured to the seat opposite him.

He could see the flicker across Lea's face. She perched on the edge of the seat, her hands clasped nervously on her lap.

He sat opposite her and put his hands on the desk. 'Lea, I have some test results we need to discuss.'

'What is it? Heart failure? Thickening?'

He shook his head. 'No, no. It's something quite different.'

Every female of child-bearing age who was a potential candidate for the research study had a whole battery of tests completed—including a pregnancy test. These were new medications, and even though they had been thoroughly researched, there were very strict rules about suitability of patients. No research study wanted to expose a growing foetus to a new type of untrialled medicine. The risks were just too high. Gene took a deep breath and kept his voice steady. 'You're pregnant.'

'I'm what?' Her voice sounded small. Almost squeaky.

For most women this would be one of the greatest moments in their life. But for Lea this had so many more repercussions.

'You're pregnant.' He said it again, keeping his voice as steady as he could. 'Obviously I'm not your normal cardiac physician, neither am I an obstetrician, and the best advice I can give you right now is that you need to speak to both.'

'I'm pregnant.' She said the words out loud again as if she was trying them for size.

Gene stood up and walked around the desk, leaning against the other side and putting his hand on her shoulder. He gave her the best supportive smile he could. He had no idea what was spinning around in her head right now.

She looked up with pale golden eyes. 'How pregnant am I?'

Gene spoke calmly. 'I can't tell you for sure.

Like I said, I'm not the expert in this, but the test results indicate around six weeks.'

She sucked in a shaky breath and he watched as a tear snaked down her cheek. She shook her head. 'I had no idea. I'm on the injection. I don't have periods. I didn't think I would get pregnant. I am always so careful—' her voice shook '—because I know the risks. I know what this can mean.'

Her hand went automatically to her stomach. 'How can I be pregnant and not even know it?'

He spoke carefully. 'Lea, you'll understand that some women don't get diagnosed with hypertrophic cardiomyopathy until they're pregnant—it doesn't get picked up until then.'

She raised her eyebrows. 'But that's not me. And I already have symptoms, I already have disease progression.' *Just like Mindy had.*

The words were instantly in his head. But he couldn't say them out loud. They wouldn't be useful right now. 'That's why you need to get some better advice. We've just done a whole range of tests on you that we are happy to share with your cardiac physician and your obstetrician.'

He hated the fact that he almost knew what they might say. Some women with hypertrophic cardiomyopathy could tolerate pregnancy. But Lea had some severe symptoms—it was why she was being considered for the research study. The blood flow through the left ventricle of her heart was extremely restricted. Could her heart really cope with the extra work that a pregnancy would entail?

That, on top of the life-threatening arrhythmias that could occur during pregnancy, would make the advice she was given at this stage crucial.

A tear slid down her face and Gene knelt in front of her. His own heart was squeezing in his chest. Right now he felt like the worst person in the world to be dealing with this. He had so much personal bias. He'd always known that through the course of his research he would likely come across patients who were pregnant with hypertrophic cardiomyopathy. He'd intentionally steered away from the studies where it seemed most likely. Not because he felt awkward but more because he wanted to always try and remain impartial, to ensure the validity of any research.

And right now? He felt anything but impartial, and that was wrong.

He reached over and put his hand over Lea's. 'I'm sorry that I had to tell you like this. And I know that for most people news of pregnancy can be a celebration. But I understand what this means for you, and I understand how much you need some advice and support right now.'

Lea stood up. It was almost as if she'd switched onto autopilot. She glanced at the notes on his desk. 'My file, can I take it for my physician?'

He nodded and picked it up. Within the institute they stored most things electronically. He'd only asked for Lea's results to be printed because he thought she might ask for the information. He followed her to the door. 'Please, ask them to get in touch. Or, if you need any help, phone us. We're happy to be of assistance.' Even he could hear the edge of desperation in his voice.

Her pale face turned towards him. 'I guess it goes without saying I'm not a candidate for the study now?'

He gave a wry shake of his head. 'I'm sorry, but no. Pregnancy excludes you from the study. We wouldn't want to risk giving you any new drugs when we have no idea what effect they could have on a growing foetus.'

She met his gaze for just a second. 'If—'

His heart almost stopped for fear of what she might say. But as soon as she started she stopped again, before she turned away and walked down the corridor.

Cordelia was walking down the corridor towards them, her bright green dress swinging as she walked. She gave a bright smile to Lea as she passed then moved swiftly over to Gene. 'I was just coming to find you—' Her words stopped abruptly as she followed his gaze to Lea's retreating figure.

'What? What's wrong?'

He shook his head and walked backwards through the door to his office again, hardly able to take his eyes from Lea's back.

Cordelia followed him. 'Gene? What is it?'

The door swung shut behind them and he leaned forward, running his hands through his hair in exasperation. 'I feel like I just let her down.'

'Who?' Cordelia glanced back over her shoulder, but at this point the only view was of the door. 'The patient?'

He nodded. 'Lea Keller. I just finished her screening for the research study.'

Cordelia's brow crinkled. 'Is something wrong? How could you let her down?'

The words were stuck somewhere in the back of his throat. He hated feeling like this. He really did. All he could think about was what might happen to Lea.

'She's pregnant.'

'Oh.' Cordelia's response came out suddenly. Quickly followed by another 'Ohh…' as she started to understand. She sucked in a deep breath. 'She's like Mindy, isn't she? Hypertrophic cardiomyopathy.'

'Hypertrophic cardiomyopathy.' Gene repeated the words. He even hated the way they sounded right now, even though he'd used the term repeatedly throughout his career, and even more so in the last four years.

'And she didn't know she was pregnant?'

Gene shook his head. 'She was on the contraceptive injection every three months. She didn't have periods and she's had no pregnancy symptoms.'

Cordelia leaned against the wall next to him. Her expression was a little glazed. 'Poor woman.' She frowned and looked at him. 'What did you tell her? '

He shook his head. 'I told her she needed to get some advice from her cardiac physician and an obstetrician. I gave her the test results and told her we were happy to help. Then I had to tell her she'd be excluded from our study.'

'But of course she will be. We can't give a pregnant woman untrialled medicines.'

He closed his eyes for a second as Lea's face flashed before him. 'She'd been quite symptomatic before. She was so keen to be part of this trial. She was hoping the new drugs would help her symptoms and improve her cardiac output.' He put one hand up to his face. 'She looked at me for just a second—and I wondered if she was going to say…'

He didn't say the words out loud, he just let them tail off.

Cordelia put her hand over his. 'You wondered if she was going to suggest she didn't continue with the pregnancy? You wondered if she was going to ask if she could still be part of the trial.'

He hated that she'd said those words out loud. He hated how they made him feel.

'What kind of doctor am I that I couldn't have that kind of conversation with her? That I couldn't allow her to think for herself, and make a decision that was right for her? It's her choice. Her decision. I know that. So why didn't I reinforce that?'

Cordelia intertwined her fingers with his and gently pulled his hand down. She stepped forward and rested her forehead against his. It was the closest they'd ever been. She spoke softly. 'Because it's not the conversation for you to have. That's for her cardiac physician—or her obstetrician. We're just the research institute, Gene. We're the temporary caregivers. For some patients we offer temporary solutions—like a sticking plaster. For others, we don't give them any benefit at all. The drugs don't work. Or they get a placebo.'

His other hand lifted up gently and rested at the back of her neck as she continued to talk.

'This isn't our conversation to have. We can't influence things like that. And you didn't. You told her to seek advice. That's exactly what you should have done.'

His voice was hoarse. 'But maybe I wasn't supportive enough. Maybe I should have been more in tune to what I felt she wanted to say. But my head was just full of Rory—and what my life would be like if Mindy had made that decision. If she'd decided not to have him—and I'd never even known about his existence. When Lea paused for a second and looked at me, that was all I could think about.'

'Stop it.' Her words were so quiet they were barely a whisper. Her warm rose-tinted scent filled his senses. 'Don't second-guess yourself. Don't put thoughts into her head that might not have been there at all. You don't know what she was thinking. And of course that might have flooded her mind for the briefest of seconds. You might be a good doctor…' her mouth curled up in a smile '…but you don't have mind-reading skills.

'She might have been wondering what to say to her partner. She might have been wondering how soon she could get an appointment to have a discussion with her cardiologist. That tiny glimmer of a second that you *thought* you saw?' Her fingers brushed against his cheek as his gaze met hers. 'It could have been nothing. It could have been nothing at all.'

She blinked and her dark eyelashes brushed against his cheek. They were *that* close, his lips less than an inch from hers. And he didn't want to move. Not for a second.

All of a sudden those glints of attraction were rolling into a giant ball that was threatening to knock him off his feet. Those cute baseball boots. The conversation with Rory on her bed. The swing of her dress. The way she sometimes bit her bottom lip as she pondered what to say next. Or even the way her dark hair had partly covered her eyes on the beach the other day.

He froze.

The touch of her fingertips was like an electric current on his skin. Those green eyes were pulling him in.

She hadn't moved an inch. For a woman

who'd at first been a little uneasy around him, he couldn't help but admire how comfortable Cordelia was in her own skin. She could have stepped back. But she hadn't. She'd moved closer and reached out.

He had to believe that she felt the same spark of attraction that he did.

He didn't want to think about it any more. Didn't want to analyse it. He didn't want to think ahead.

She was looking straight at him. He murmured gently, 'Someone once told me that research has proved that if you take just a little of what you crave, it makes management much easier.'

Her lips curled into a smile. 'I wonder who that could have been,' she breathed. 'I think I might agree with them.'

He didn't hesitate for another moment, just leaned down and captured her lips with his.

For a second he held his breath, waiting to see if she would object. But she didn't. He could almost sense her smiling again as they kissed, her lips matching his. The rose scent surrounded him as his hand slid up from the back of her neck and through her silky tresses. Her hand stayed on his cheek as they kissed, her touch light as her other hand lay on his chest.

She tasted of strawberries and sunshine. He pulled her closer and her warm curves pressed against the hard planes of his body. They were at work. Anyone could open the office door at any moment. He was just a visiting researcher. This job was Cordelia's life.

She let out a little sigh and it was almost his undoing. He wanted nothing more than to walk her backwards to the desk behind them and push her on to it.

But Cordelia would never be that kind of girl. And he wasn't really that kind of guy. As other parts of his body started to respond he took a deep breath and pulled back. He couldn't help the smile that plastered its way across his face. His breathing was hard. Her hands rested on his shoulders.

'Wow,' came the quiet voice.

'Wow,' he echoed.

For a second they just stood there, then a nervous kind of laugh bubbled up inside her, and she made herself step back out of his embrace, her breathing a little stuttered.

He raised his hand, but she shook her head. 'Don't. Don't say anything. We both know that you're only here for a month, and that Rory has to be your priority.'

Confusion swept over his face. 'But—'

It was the oddest feeling. She spent her life trying so much to achieve control. In her work life. In her personal life. And in all other aspects.

The arrhythmias were the only thing she'd partly accepted as not being within her control—but that didn't stop her trying her absolute best to keep a handle on things. She hated that it might affect her work. She'd prefer people at work didn't know about it. Didn't need sympathetic glances. And she really didn't want her fellow professionals constantly asking her about living with the condition.

Her reasons for her research were her own.

So this didn't help. This wave of emotions threatening to overcome her made her want to run a mile.

How could one kiss do this to her? Or was it one kiss, and the near miss the other day?

Or was it everything? Living under the same roof as Gene and Rory. Watching the relationship between father and son. Or was it being exposed to such a gorgeous, sweet-natured, fun-loving child? Realising that she would never have that relationship with a child. She'd never have that gift.

Or was it all just pure Gene—pure cowboy? Taking one look at a sexy Texan with the form-fitting jeans, broad chest and come-to-bed eyes?

She started. Where had that thought come from? Heat rushed into her cheeks.

Gene touched her hand and she flinched, then almost cringed.

She couldn't pretend not to see the flicker of hurt on his face. 'Maybe I should go,' he said throatily. 'I guess I read things wrong. I'm sorry if I did.'

The lump in her throat was the size of a tennis ball. But she couldn't let him walk out here like that.

They were still living under the same roof. She still had to see him every day at work.

'You didn't.' She held up her hands, not quite sure of was the right thing to say. The last thing Gene needed was her whole heap of rambling thoughts.

Her feet seemed rooted to the spot. The words bumbled around in her head. This was where she should say something really smart. But her brain refused.

He'd moved closer to the door, the hurt look still on his face.

She struggled to find the words.

'You didn't,' she repeated, then held out her arms. 'It's just…it's here. It's work. I just don't feel comfortable doing this at work.'

He blinked. Then hesitated, then nodded. 'Of course.'

But he didn't smile. He opened the door. 'We can talk later.'

He nodded and walked out.

Awkwardness and relief hit her at once.

She'd just experienced the best kiss in her lifetime.

With the sexiest guy she'd ever met.

She should be shouting from the rooftops.

But all she could think about was how this

didn't feel right. *She* didn't feel right. She didn't want to start something that had the potential to be wonderful.

Not when she was keeping secrets.

Not when her heart felt so at risk.

Control was rapidly slipping through her fingers—a sensation she wasn't familiar with.

But, if that kiss was anything to go by, the one thing she truly knew was that by the time she reached home tonight all bets were off.

CHAPTER SEVEN

THE CALL CAME at seven p.m., just as he was about to leave work and pick up Rory from an outing with the institute nursery. He frowned at the phone number, thinking the last few digits were familiar. But this was an international call. Who would be looking for him?

'Gene Du Bois?'

'Gene? It's Franc. Franc Helier.'

'Professor Helier?' It was odd. But Gene naturally defaulted into Franc's professional title. Although they'd spoken on many occasions before he'd got the job, he'd never actually had the pleasure of meeting Franc. And Gene had been brought up strictly—he couldn't quite bring himself to call the professor by his first name.

'Yes, yes, it's me.'

'How are you? How are things with your sister? I was sorry to hear that she was unwell.'

There was silence for a second. Then a small

sniff. Gene cringed. Maybe it would have been better not to say anything, but it seemed rude not to acknowledge Professor Helier's family issues.

'Yes, yes…well, not really. Things aren't particularly good. I'm going to have to stay a bit longer—maybe a lot longer.' There was a deep sigh. 'In fact, I have no idea at all how long I need to stay. It could be days, it could be months. All I know is I have to be here.'

He could hear the stress and strain in Franc's voice. 'Of course, Professor, of course you have to stay. What can I do to help?'

His offer came out automatically—just the way his mother would have expected.

'Actually… I know it's a terrible imposition. And I know you have family commitments. And I know your contract is only for a month, but—'

Gene cut in. 'But you want to know if I'll stay.'

He could hear the whoosh of relief. 'Yes,' said Professor Helier quickly. 'Would you be able to?'

Normally, when faced with a decision like

this, Gene would think carefully, consider all the options, and take into account all his plans—for himself and for Rory. But for the first time in his life he really didn't need to think for long—it only took a few seconds.

'I will. The truth is I love the research I'm doing here. I think there's a real chance of making a difference for patients with cardiomyopathy. I'd love to stay here for longer and continue with the studies.'

'You would? Really?' The excitement and relief was clear in the professor's voice.

'I would,' said Gene with a nod of his head. He meant it. He really did. Rory seemed happy. He liked the institute. He liked the work. He liked the people. Probably one in particular...

He gave himself a shake. 'What about Cordelia? Have you discussed this with her?'

The professor gave a little cough. 'I'm just about to. But I wanted to ask you first if you would consider staying. If you'd said it was impossible, then I would have had to ask Cordelia to advertise for a replacement. I'm so glad I don't have to do that.'

Gene gave another nod of his head. 'You don't.

I had tentatively accepted an offer to work elsewhere. But that can be changed. I don't have any commitments back at home for a few months, when Rory is due to start at school.'

'So there could be more flexibility if needed?' Professor Helier's voice was a little high-pitched.

Gene took a deep breath. He wasn't quite ready to set down roots, but he could only imagine the stress Professor Helier was under. His sister was clearly very sick and couldn't be left. So Gene did what his mother would expect him to do. 'There can be. Let's talk again in another month.'

'Thank you, Dr Du Bois. I can't thank you enough for this. I'll phone Cordelia now and let her know the change in arrangements.'

Gene's heart gave a little lift in his chest as he finished the call.

It really was odd. Normally, something like this would have made him consider all his options, look at all things carefully. He didn't usually ever make snap decisions like this. Today he hadn't had to do that at all. Not for a second.

Something was changing. And he had a sneaking suspicion he knew why.

* * *

By the time Gene had manoeuvred Rory into his pyjamas and into his own bed the small boy had woken up again.

Rory had been exhausted after the outing with the nursery and had fallen asleep in the car on the journey home. Gene had been glad of the quiet to contemplate what he'd just done—and the effect it might have.

The buzz between him and Cordelia was so intense he could swear he could almost see the electricity in the air. There was no denying it—just looking at her made him smile, then within a few seconds look away again because his mind was filled with a wave of attraction so strong he might want to act on it.

All he could think about was that kiss today. Things had been left a little awkward, with that whole aspect of what might come next.

And he couldn't wait to find out what that might be.

By the time he'd walked out the shower, Rory had wandered through to Gene's room, rubbing his sleepy eyes.

Gene quickly dried himself with a towel then

picked Rory up and sat up on the bed with him. He felt a pang of frustration. And it made him angry with himself.

Angry for being a normal human male and realising whatever he might have hoped for in the next hour or so had probably just been curtailed.

He'd kept Rory so separate from his love life that he'd never had to think like this before. On the rare occasions he'd dated, he'd always had safe and reliable arrangements in place for Rory. His father loved having his grandson and showing the little guy around the ranch. And he'd also encouraged Gene to get out there and find someone. 'You can't stop living. Yes, you can be a great dad and prioritise your son. But that doesn't stop you having relationships.' He'd even winked at Gene. 'I'd actually prefer it if you did, means I get to see more of my grandson.'

But there were only a few people Gene would trust with his son. His dad, or his brother and his wife, and one of his mother's best friends in Paris. It wasn't easy to plan dates around Paris and Texas, so this was the first time he'd actually been put in a position where he wanted to actually meet someone and spend some alone time with them, but couldn't do it.

He hated feeling like that. He really did.

'Dad?'

At this point Rory was huddled underneath his arm. 'What is it?'

'At nursery, Pim got a new mom.'

The hairs on his body bristled. Where on earth had this come from?

'You found this out today?'

'No, yesterday,' came the far-off little voice.

Gene swallowed. Had this been preying on his son's mind?

'What do you mean—Pim got a new mom?'

'Pim's mom went away. But now he's getting a new one. He doesn't like her. She smells funny.'

Gene's stifled his automatic reaction to the kid's words. From the mouths of babes. Rory twisted under his arm and looked up with his sleepy dark eyes. His voice was quiet. 'If I get a new mom, can I pick her?'

Gene's heart squeezed in his chest. 'Of course you can pick her. A new mom is a big deal. It's really always just been the two of us. We'd have to think long and hard before we decided if we wanted a girl to join us.' He knew he probably shouldn't make light of this conversation, but how did you have this kind of conversation with a kid this age?

He'd always told himself he would be as open and honest with Rory as possible. He wanted to think that in future years Rory would feel as if he could talk to him about anything. But the truth was, it was harder than he'd ever figured.

He squeezed Rory under his arm as the little head lay down on his belly. 'We're a team, sport, we're in this together—a package deal.'

'Good,' murmured Rory, ''cause I pick Delia.'

Gene froze, his stomach tensing. Had he just heard correctly?

Goosebumps appeared on his skin. It was like a million little caterpillars stomping all over his chest.

Almost instantly Rory was semi-snoring.

His breath had hitched itself somewhere inside his chest. He blew it out in one long slow moment.

He'd been so wound up about himself, about his attraction to Cordelia that he'd failed to notice something with his son. Rory was growing attached. He'd never really had a mother figure around him. Was he starting to imagine Cordelia in that role? Because this wasn't exactly where Gene's brain had been.

He tried to put himself in his four-year-old's mind. Another kid had just said he was getting a new mom and didn't like her. That was a big deal. Huge. So Rory had thought about the first female he'd actually formed a sort of relationship with—and liked. Cordelia. Was that really such a big deal?

He was blowing this out of proportion. He was taking a four-year-old's glimmer of appreciation, along with the child's simplistic view of picking a new mom. He needed to stop and think sensibly.

This wasn't really about Rory. This was about his unexpected attraction to Cordelia.

This was ridiculous. He was a grown man. True, he was experiencing his first real attraction in a long time. True, this wasn't ideal circumstances or timing. He ruffled Rory's hair. His son would always be number one. His priority.

But did that mean he had to ignore everything

else? He was in charge of his own destiny. The attraction was mutual. He wasn't dumb. And he wanted to act on it. *Really* wanted to act on it.

He took another breath and slid Rory gently to the side, arranging the covers around him.

He kissed him on the forehead and pulled on some clothes. 'Wish me luck,' he whispered as he headed for the door.

Cordelia found herself pacing around the kitchen. She'd showered, washed her hair, then hovered around her doorway, wondering what to do next.

That kiss four hours ago had put her on edge. What next? Was Gene having the same thoughts she was?

He couldn't be. If he was, he'd have turned up at her door.

She flicked the switch on the kettle, changed her mind and pulled out a wine glass instead. Her fingers slipped on the wine bottle as she tried to push in the corkscrew. 'Darn it,' she murmured. A few seconds later a pair of hands covered hers, and she felt a warm body behind hers. She shivered.

'Let me help you with that,' said the husky voice.

It was like music to her ears.

His hands were deft, bare arms next to hers as he popped the cork from the wine, then let a hand slide around her waist as he moved to the side.

'So, are we having wine?' he asked as she pulled another glass from the cupboard.

She licked her bottom lip as she turned to face him. She could almost hear her heartbeat thudding in her ears. 'I wasn't sure if you'd join me.' The words were simple. But it was the boldest thing she could say.

He lifted the bottle and poured the wine achingly slowly into both glasses, before lifting his towards her. 'I guess I wondered if I should.'

Her stomach knotted tightly. But he continued, 'I've never really taken things further when Rory is around. He's never met anyone that I've dated.'

'We're dating?' She picked up the glass and took a sip before smiling at him. It was ridiculous. She was standing in her satin nightdress, short nightgown, and very bare legs. She felt a flutter in her chest. No way. Not now. Not here.

But after a second she realised it was nothing.

She almost laughed out loud. She was normal. Her heart was just skipping a few beats—the way it did for the whole world over when they were swamped with hormones and adrenaline.

He gave her a sexy kind of smile. 'I think we could almost call today our first date.'

'Is office kisses the kind of date you normally go on with women?'

His brow wrinkled as his fingers spread out a little at her waist. If she didn't know better, she'd think he was going to pull her closer.

He gave a soft laugh and met her gaze. The look he gave her almost took her breath away. Open, sincere and sexy as hell.

'Okay. Let's call the day out together our first date then. I think I've just started a new form of dating. No one I've dated has met Rory before. I like to keep those two parts of my life separate.'

She moved forward, letting her body press against his. She tilted her head to one side. 'And now?'

He nodded slowly and set his wine glass down, running the fingers of one hand through her hair. 'I guess it's time to try something new.'

She licked her lips again. 'I hear that you're staying.'

A smile danced around his lips. 'I might have been persuaded to stay.'

She raised her eyebrows. 'Persuaded? By what?'

He raised his eyebrows too. 'Maybe it's not a what. Maybe…it's a who.'

Now he pulled her towards him, the hard planes of his chest against her soft breasts, his lips at her neck as he whispered in her ear, 'Now, this something new. Want to try it with me?'

She set down her glass before it fell over and let her head tip back, exposing her neck to his lips. He didn't need any more of an invitation.

If the kiss in the office had been passionate, this one was different. This one was slow, taunting and teasing her, his lips almost tickling her skin, making her arch towards him and beg for more.

Her arms closed around his shoulders, tightening their grip on him. 'I guess we all should learn something new,' she whispered, her voice barely able to form the words. 'Didn't I tell you before? Every day is a new day, with a world of possibilities,' she breathed.

He laughed. 'I like the sound of that.' He bent down and swept her up in his arms. 'My room is taken.' He grinned cheekily at her. 'Looks like it'll have to be yours.'

She couldn't stop the smile. 'What are you waiting for?' she urged as the kitchen disappeared behind them.

CHAPTER EIGHT

THE NEXT FEW weeks passed in a blur. Cordelia had never really been quite so happy. The research was going well. They were moving closer and closer to being able to replicate the abilities of the zebrafish. Everything at the institute seemed to be running smoothly.

And everything at home seemed to be better than she could have possibly hoped for. The truth was, her apartment had now been fixed and she could move back anytime she wanted.

But she didn't want to.

She was enjoying staying at Professor Helier's house with Gene and Rory. They'd fallen into some kind of easy routine. She knew it wasn't permanent but that didn't seem to matter too much.

All that mattered was, for the first time in forever, she actually felt happy. She was getting to enjoy the experience of developing a relationship with the sexiest guy she'd ever met, and the cutest little boy.

Every day that she sat at the table, buttering toast for Rory and drinking coffee with Gene, made her happy, and a tiny bit sad.

Professor Helier's sister was deteriorating little by little. No one knew when she would die— only that at some point it would be inevitable.

And at that point he would return to the institute and Gene and Rory would leave. That made her insides twist in a way she didn't like.

Gene appeared in the doorway at her office just as she was trying to contemplate how quiet things would be for her once they had gone. 'Are you ready?'

She smiled but frowned. 'Ready for what?'

He shook his head, folded his arms and leaned on the doorjamb. 'Marie and I actually had a bet that you might forget.'

She stood up quickly. If he'd been talking to Marie it must be something about work. She started riffling through some of the papers on her desk.

'Watch out,' came the playful voice. 'You're

in danger of turning into Professor Helier with a desk like that.'

She looked down and laughed. 'You're right. But I'll have you know that *his* desk and office is immaculate. I've tidied it up but...' she blew some hair from her face '...transferred the stuff I've still to deal with to my desk.'

Gene walked towards her. 'Anything interesting?'

She bit her lip for a second, wondering how much to say. 'Well...yes.' She picked up two folders, one green, one blue. 'There are two really interesting research proposals for next year.'

Gene was instantly interested. 'What are they?'

She had a pang of regret. Chances were he was hoping it was another cardiomyopathy research trial. It was likely there would be one, but neither of these fitted the bill. She didn't have anything in her hand that might persuade him to stay.

She spoke quickly. 'One is around Marfan syndrome and the impact on the aorta and heart, and one is around Wolff-Parkinson-White syndrome, heart regeneration and renewal pathways.' The pang plucked even deeper. Franc hadn't discussed this with her. He knew how much she would want to campaign for this study—even if she wasn't directly overseeing it.

'Those sound great, really interesting. What stage are they at?'

He bent over to take one of the files from her hand. He had no idea which would be which, so she was relieved when he took the blue file and started flicking through it. He read for a few moments then looked up, nodding thoughtfully, 'I can see where Franc's made notes about the research study, the ethics and practicalities.' He wrinkled his brow. 'He couldn't have had a chance to send his notes back.'

He tucked the blue folder containing the proposal regarding Marfan's syndrome under his arm. 'Tell you what, why don't you let me send Franc's notes back to the proposer for this study, and you do it for the other one. It will probably take them a few weeks to gather all the extra details needed.' He gave a broad smile. 'Let's not leave them hanging.'

She nodded quickly. 'Sure, why not? That seems fair.'

He was still smiling at her.

'What?' she asked.

'You have forgotten, haven't you?'

He walked around the desk towards her and slid an arm around her waist.

'Is this work-related?'

He shook his head. 'Look at your watch.'

She glanced down and looked at her watch. 'What?'

He sighed. 'I'm beginning to think you're playing hard to get.'

She slid her arms around his neck and kissed him. 'Me? Hard to get with you? I think we can safely say that's not happening.'

He glanced down at her baseball boots. 'Cordelia Greenway, we might get into the cinema with those boots, but if you want to go to that fancy restaurant, we might be in trouble.'

The penny dropped. 'Of course!' Her hand flew up to her mouth. 'That's today?'

Because Gene was reluctant to leave Rory with anyone he didn't really know, they'd both agreed to have a day date instead of an evening one. That way Rory could stay in the institute nursery with staff that he knew and they could catch a movie and have an early dinner together. It was unusual. Most of the time they'd been together, Rory had been included in all their plans, but Gene seemed to be keen they have a little adult time too—and not just in the bedroom.

She cringed. 'Sorry, I've spent all day thinking this was Tuesday.'

He was still smiling, his hands on both her hips. 'Nope, it's Wednesday all day today.' He whispered in her ear, 'Get your coat, you've pulled.'

She burst out laughing. They'd spent the day before talking about bad pick-up lines. 'Okay.' She looked down at her red baseball boots. 'I have a pair of heels under my desk. I can take them with me for our early dinner.'

Gene proffered his elbow towards her. 'Come on, then, Cordelia. Let's go be grown-ups for a while—because by the time we get home tonight, it will be dinosaur movies all the way.'

She was dedicated to her work. He admired that in her. So he hadn't been the least bit offended that she'd forgotten their date.

Ten minutes later she was ready, heels in her large bag that seemed to hold the entire contents of the world. They walked the picturesque road from the institute hand in hand. For the first few days Cordelia had been a little shy about letting anyone know about their relationship. But she'd gradually relaxed—which was just as well, since it had only taken a few days for the rest of the staff to work it out.

He swore she almost glowed right now. Her steps seemed lighter, her mood brighter, and what made him happiest was how hard she worked to include Rory in everything. Even though she'd been a little awkward around him initially, the hesitancy had left her and she seemed to have almost warmed to her role around Rory.

She'd mentioned she didn't have brothers or sisters, so she had no nieces or nephews. Maybe she just hadn't had much exposure to young kids? Whatever it was, it was gone now. And for that Gene was grateful.

'What's it to be? Are you an action fan? Sci-fi?' She gave a laugh. 'Or what about romance? Everyone loves romance.'

They were approaching the large cinema complex adorned with multiple posters advertising a wide range of movies. Gene stopped in front of the first advertisement. It was a hopeless romance. He turned to Cordelia, 'Okay, so you know that I like you, don't you?'

She rolled her eyes in the cutest possible way. 'Like? Okay, I'm about to go all teenager and stomp off.' There was a real twinkle in her eye.

He let out a mock sigh as he slung his arm around her shoulders and pulled her close. 'Okay, so *more* than like. But no matter how much I more than like you, we're not going to see that movie.'

She laughed as she put her hand on his chest as she looked up at the poster. She shook her head. 'That's fine.' She pointed to the hero. 'He's not my favourite, anyway.'

Gene raised his eyebrows. 'Just as well.' He kept smiling as they walked along to the next one. An action movie about racing. He shook his head. 'Not much story in this one.'

The next one looked more promising. 'So, Dr Greenway, how do you feel about a little sci-fi?'

Cordelia looked thoughtful. 'An adventure set

in space with a kick-ass heroine?' She nodded and held out her hand towards him. 'I think I can be persuaded.'

Three hours later they emerged from the cinema into the still bright afternoon sunshine. Gene's lips were almost numb. He'd spent a good part of the movie kissing the woman in his arms. It was like being a teenager again. Ridiculous.

They headed to the French-style restaurant he'd booked earlier that week and Cordelia leaned on his shoulder as she quickly changed her shoes and straightened her skirt and blouse to make herself look more respectable. She looked up at him with bright eyes. 'How do I look?'

He leaned forward and kissed her red lips. 'Perfect—like always.'

She laughed as he held the door open for her and entered the restaurant.

Although it was early, the lights were dim, setting an ambience that was just right.

They ordered some wine and took the recommendations from the maître d'. The restaurant was quiet and he liked it that way, because it gave them some privacy.

'How are you feeling? You look a little pale.'

She wrinkled her nose. 'Do I? I guess I am a little tired, but nothing else.' She gave a grin. 'Maybe it's the unexpected late nights.'

He nodded. 'Could be. Rory seems to like it here. He's settled really well.'

Cordelia winced a little. 'How will that be when you move on?'

He couldn't help but raise an eyebrow. 'Trying to get rid of us?' He hated the way his stomach gave a flip.

She shook her head. 'Of course not. I like having you here.' She picked up her wine glass. 'Or maybe I just like having Rory.' She laughed. 'He's definitely more obedient.'

The waiter brought over their entrées.

Gene hesitated for a second. He was curious about Cordelia. He still had the impression there were things he didn't really know. For a start, she was one of the smartest, prettiest doctors he'd ever met. He couldn't help but be surprised that some other guy hadn't swept her off her feet.

'I'm glad you and Rory have hit it off,' he said carefully as he picked up his knife and fork. 'It kind of makes me wonder whether you'd ever considered having a family of your own? Would you consider kids in your future?'

It was bold. It was downright nosy. But he was finding himself more drawn to Cordelia every day. He'd accepted the chance to stay here easily. Would he consider staying longer? What if Professor Helier decided to work on both of those new studies next year? He would need assistance—a lead researcher for each. Would it really be such a hardship for him to consider some other form of cardiac research besides cardiomyopathy?

He looked up sharply as Cordelia gave a little cough, as if she'd choked on her chicken entrée. Her face had paled.

'Cordelia, are you okay? Do you need some water?'

She shook her head sharply, hand at her throat as she looked down at her plate. The paleness disappeared quickly as colour rushed into her cheeks.

She waited a few moments before she answered the earlier question. 'I've never really considered having children. It's never been on my radar. I haven't met the right guy and all that,' she added dismissively.

There was a strangeness in her tone. Something decidedly forced. It sent a prickle down his spine.

It was every woman's right to choose if she wanted to have children or not, but somehow her answer wasn't that convincing. 'Children weren't on my radar either, at least not until I knew Rory existed. I guess at some point in the distant future I thought I might have a family. But sometimes life has other plans for us.'

He looked up into her green eyes. She blinked sharply, her eyes glassy.

'Yeah,' she muttered. 'I guess life does that.'

He probably shouldn't pursue it. But every part of his curiosity was spiked. 'So you never met the right guy, huh? No one you ever wanted to engaged to or married to?'

She pulled her shoulders back. 'That's an awfully traditional view. Does a woman have to be engaged or married? Can't she just be happy on her own?' She sounded remarkably defensive—almost as if she'd taken offence at his words.

'Are you happy on your own?'

She bristled. 'I've managed to get through the last thirty-one years on my own. It's amazing how self-sufficient we women can be.'

Gene cringed. This wasn't at all how he'd wanted the conversation to go. He'd been trying to sound Cordelia out about her plans for the future, not to make her instantly annoyed and defensive.

He paused. 'I don't doubt your self-sufficiency, Cordelia. I would never question that.' He hoped his tone was softer than before. 'I just wondered if you had any plans for the future.'

She paused again. He could almost swear she looked as if she had tears in her eyes. How on earth could he cause so much upset by just asking a basic question? Wasn't it normal for people who were dating to have this kind of conversation after a while? He'd kind of hoped that Cordelia might eventually want the same kind of future that he did. She seemed to get on well with Rory. Had he imagined that? Was it so wrong that he might a picture a future he could spend with the woman he loved, his son and maybe another child?

Something twisted inside him. It seemed like everything was going wrong here.

Her expression was pained. 'Of course I have plans for the future. There's new research and—'

'I wasn't talking about work.' He knew he'd cut her off, but she was about to start babbling. She hadn't really done that since they'd first met.

'What exactly were you talking about, then?' she snapped.

His appetite gone, he pushed his plate away and reached across the table and took her hand. 'I was talking about us, Cordelia. I wondered what might happen next.'

He stared at her shocked expression.

'But you'll have to leave. You've said that yourself.'

He nodded. 'I know I have. But if Professor Helier is taking on new projects, he might be looking for someone to lead one.'

'But neither of the new projects is to do with cardiomyopathy.'

He pulled one hand back and ran it through his hair with a sigh. 'I know I said that I only wanted to look at cardiomyopathy because of Rory. And I suppose I do. But now I guess I'm considering if I want to widen my interests in cardiac research.'

She blinked. 'Because of me? Because of us?'

He took a long, slow breath. What he'd hoped might be a light conversation that might help him sort out the thoughts in his head had turned into almost a declaration of his intentions. Was he ready for this?

Cordelia's reaction hadn't been what he'd expected. Why so defensive? Maybe he was completely misreading the situation.

'Maybe,' he replied. 'I'd always intended to take Rory back to Texas or Paris to start school—mainly because I have people there that I trust with my son. I never really thought about any alternatives.'

She wasn't saying anything. She wasn't giving him any reason to think he should stay.

Her voice came out in a squeak. 'And now you are?'

Frustration was building in him. The waiter

appeared and removed their plates, his mouth twisting once he saw how little they'd eaten.

Gene leaned back in his chair. The words *I was* ran through his brain. But he could hardly say that out loud now.

'I guess I just wanted to know if you had plans for the future.' He waved his hand. 'For all I know, you might have decided you wanted to leave the institute and work someplace else. You might have decided you don't want to be a researcher any more and have plans to move to the jungle in Borneo and study plant life.' He knew how ridiculous this sounded, but it wasn't just about him, it was about Rory too, so he had to put it out there.

He sighed and looked at her. There seemed to be an air of panic about her. He hadn't expected that—not after how well things had been going between them. 'I don't want to uproot my life and my son if you can't see any plans with us in them.'

It was the most exposed Gene had felt since Mindy had died. Since Karen had walked out.

It was out there. He'd said it. He'd put his cards on the table. The waiter reappeared and put down their main courses, fussing around them until Gene almost snapped.

Cordelia still hadn't spoken.

When she did, her voice wavered. 'Well, I've no plans to go to Borneo—or anyplace else for that matter. I've always thought about my future being here at the institute. When I got here, it just felt like home.' Her fingers twiddled nervously with a bit of hair. 'I've had a few other tentative job offers, but I've never even considered them.'

She wasn't meeting his gaze. She was looking everywhere but at him.

'This was a bad idea. I shouldn't have said anything.' What he really wanted to do was push his chair back, stand up and leave. The light, airy restaurant was suddenly feeling claustrophobic.

Her voice was quiet. 'No. You should have.' She gave a half-smile. It was first time he felt as if her barriers fell a little. 'I guess I just wasn't quite prepared for it.'

A wave of sadness washed over him. He felt like some high school guy who'd just asked out the popular girl and been turned down. 'Well, if you weren't prepared for it, I think we're both in different places. I'm sorry if I put you on the spot. I'm sorry if I made you uncomfortable.'

His insides were curling up and dying.

But Cordelia shook her head quickly. 'No. No. We're not really in different places. I just… I just hadn't contemplated that you might change your plans. I kind of thought they would be set in stone. You're so clear about what you want for Rory. I never hoped or imagined you might change your mind.'

It was first flicker of hope that she'd given him. Had he really seemed so single-minded?

She put her hand up to her chest and kept talking. 'Of course I was delighted when you stayed a little longer. And I know Franc will come back, but I also know he's getting older. He needs more help, more support. I think he'll always want to be Head of the Institute. He loves the place. It's his life. But if he could have me lead on one side, and someone else like you lead on the other? It would be such a weight off him.'

She was babbling. But this time he didn't stop her. He needed to hear what she had to say.

She looked around, as if checking to see if

anyone was listening to her, as she leaned across the table towards him. 'Gene, I love having you around. I love having Rory around. I haven't been this happy in…well, for ever.' She gave a sad kind of smile. 'But in my head I never hoped you'd want to hang around because of me. I just thought that wanting any more would line me up for heartache.'

Now he was getting somewhere.

Neither of them had said the other word. The one that was like an elephant in the room. And Gene wasn't sure he was ready, even though he couldn't deny his brain and heart were walking down that path.

'You think I could cause you heartache?' His teasing tone lightened the tense mood a little.

She threw down her napkin. 'Phew, I bet you were the regular heartbreak kid in Paris and Texas while you were at school. It's practically written all over your face.'

He almost laughed out loud. 'I might have had a few girlfriends at school.'

Now she shook her head. 'A few!' she mocked. 'You were the kind of guy that girls wrote about on bathroom walls.'

He leaned forward, stretching out his fingers to touch her hand again. 'Have you written about me on any bathroom walls?'

This time their gazes meshed. All he could see were her bright green eyes, clear skin and shiny dark hair. 'Not yet.' She smiled. 'It's a work thing. You know, it's hard trying to resist defacing the walls of the women's bathroom in the institute.'

The waiter hovered around them, looking at their almost full plates disdainfully.

'We're fine,' said Gene quickly. 'Can you give us some more time, please?'

He sucked in a deep breath and lifted up his glass of wine. 'How about we agree to see how things develop. I don't want you to feel as if I'm pushing something. I just wanted to be honest. To put my cards on the table.'

She nodded and lifted her glass to his. 'That sounds good. That sounds…nice.'

He raised his eyebrows. 'Nice?' The possibility of their relationship developing was nice? Should he run for the hills now?

She clinked her glass against his. 'What can I say? Too many people around.'

But the smile she had on her face told him all he really wanted. She looked happy. The tension had left her neck and shoulders. She finally looked as relaxed as she had earlier.

But somewhere inside his stomach gave a little flip.

He'd started the day so positively, and now? He just wasn't sure.

Gene wanted to stay. He wanted to stay because of *her*.

While that made her heart swell in her chest, it also made her feel sick.

She hadn't been honest with him. She hadn't told him about her condition. It wasn't that she'd really meant to hide it. It was just that she was quite a private person. And at first she hadn't been sure how long he would be here, and hadn't wanted him to feel sorry for her.

But now…it was something else. It was a secret. Something she hadn't shared. And she felt slightly dishonest.

He was looking to the future. Would he want to have a relationship with a woman who had a cardiac condition? Particularly one that had ruled out the possibility of children?

Because that's what he'd been asking. He'd been asking her if she'd contemplated having children.

Had she contemplated it? She'd done more than that. She'd ached with loneliness and cried long, hard tears after realising that getting pregnant could put herself and her baby at risk. She'd already had one man leave her because she couldn't have kids. She certainly couldn't take the heartbreak of another. Because this time it was different. She hadn't felt this way about Han. Their relationship had been sweet. Comfortable. But her heart hadn't skipped in her chest when she'd heard his voice, or felt his touch. Not the way it did with Gene.

As for having children? For a few years she'd been obsessed. The whole world around her had seemed to be expecting a baby. Friends, workmates and old university colleagues all seemed to be simultaneously pregnant.

Accepting what was for the best had been hard. She'd moved into self-protect mode, taking cautious steps away from friends who rapidly had one baby after another, and throwing herself into her work.

She couldn't pretend it hadn't stopped her forming new relationships. She'd really never wanted to have that conversation out loud. To finally say the words *I'm sorry, I can't have children*, and be met with a look of disappointment. In her head it would inevitably lead to the breakdown of any relationship, and she just didn't want that. She didn't want to feel as if she lacked something.

And she always knew she would never do that to someone she loved—ask them to give up the thing she longed for too. It wouldn't be fair.

So she'd tried to take herself out of those equations. And now?

Gene had the most adorable little boy on the planet. But it was clear he was interested in having more.

She would have to tell him. No matter how much she didn't want to.

But the truth was, a little part of her heart was still singing. Singing at the part of life that had led them to meet. Had put them under the same roof, and let her meet this gorgeous Texan and his son.

He thought she was worth it. Wasn't that what he'd implied? That he'd consider changing his plans and stay here with her?

A single tear snaked down her face as she towel-dried her hair in the bathroom. They'd picked up Rory and come home to spend the evening together. Rory wanted to be a couch potato. So they were all putting in their pyjamas and getting ready to watch the latest kids' movie with cowboys and spacemen.

Part of her wanted to stay in this bathroom and cry. She'd made a mess of things today. He'd asked her about plans for the future and all the words she should have said had jumbled around in her brain and completely stuck in her throat.

She knew what she should have said.

But her brain just couldn't go there.

Part of her heart had been leaping around in her chest—threatening a WPW attack any moment. But deep down in her soul she was pining already.

Pining for this gorgeous man and his son.

She couldn't pretend they could be a family together—not when Gene seemed to have hopes to expand their family.

At some point in the near future she'd have to tell him the truth—that she had Wolff-Parkinson-White syndrome. That her symptoms were so severe her cardiologist had strongly advised against ever considering getting pregnant. She knew there were a lot of women with the condition who tolerated pregnancy without too many complications. But everyone was different.

And she was different from most.

She brushed the tears away from her face and tugged a comb through her hair roughly. Gene had been here six weeks ago. He could be here much longer. Was it so wrong to keep pretending? To have a little of the life she really wanted?

She might never get this chance again. To love someone. To be loved.

She pressed her lips together. If he mentioned staying again—if he started to make plans—she could tell him then.

She wouldn't let him find out from anyone

else. But she could have a few weeks. A few weeks of the almost perfect life.

A few more weeks of the most gorgeous cowboy and his adorable son.

She loved the sideways glances from Gene when his mouth said one thing but his eyes hinted at a whole lot more. She loved the way Rory flung his arms around her neck and bearhugged her. She wanted it to last just a little bit longer.

If she told Gene, and he considered still working at the institute, then she would deal with that. It was highly likely he wouldn't want to continue their relationship.

But that didn't mean he would disappear to Paris or Texas. He liked it here. Chances were that Franc would need the support they'd discussed. Franc had already been impressed by Gene's résumé. He might well offer him a permanent position.

But if he stayed, could she watch Gene fall in love with someone else and build his family?

It didn't bear thinking about.

She shook her head, demanding the tears forming in her eyes disappear.

She was taking this time. She was taking it.

The next few weeks were hers. She wanted to laugh. She wanted to enjoy.

And if she lost her heart in the process, to not one guy but two?

Then it was a cross she would just have to bear.

CHAPTER NINE

HER GAZE FLICKERED to the view outside. On the path outside the institute a woman was walking with a stroller. The little girl in the stroller had a mass of dark curls and was wearing a bright red coat and a pair of black patent-leather shoes. It reminded Cordelia of a photograph of herself when she was around two. Who knew those curls would tame into poker-straight hair?

A wave of unease crept down her spine and she swallowed uncomfortably. Something sparked in her brain.

She reached for her bag as she hurried inside the institute and fumbled to find her hand-held diary. It had to be in here somewhere. Pens, her mobile phone, receipts, credit-card wallet, umbrella and foldaway bag, along with the odd chocolate all ended up dumped on her office desk.

She didn't stop to repack. She flicked through

the pages quickly as the prickle of unease spread like the march of a legion of soldiers over her skin.

She pushed her wheeled chair closer to the wall, where there was a large calendar. Her head flicked between the calendar and her diary.

No. No.

Her hand went to her throat, her mouth instantly dry.

Her period was late. Her fingers flicked through the pages again, as if they could find a mistake. Cold sweat broke out on her skin. She leaned back in the chair, staring out the windows towards the snow-topped Alps.

Had she been careless? No. She hadn't. Years ago she'd accepted what pregnancy could do to her body and she'd always been meticulous about her method of contraception. Her IUD had been securely in place for a while. She hadn't been sick. She hadn't been taken antibiotics. Nothing had changed. Everything should be fine.

She let out a groan. Of course everything had changed. Gene was here, and for the last few weeks he'd been in her bed.

She'd been under more pressure at work while Franc was gone, she'd been…distracted, to say the least, with her change in personal circumstances.

Bile rose in the back of her throat. Right now she could be sick all over her shoes. She'd need to tell him. She'd need to tell him about her WPW condition and what this could likely mean.

The implications had always been there for her. She'd known about them right from the start. But Gene? He knew nothing about this and, what's worse, he'd already been through this once.

What kind of a person was she? Why hadn't she spoken to him right at the start?

Now it wasn't a prickle of unease. Now it was heading towards a full-blown panic attack.

As if in penance for her behaviour, her heart started beating erratically. She pulled her chair over to the desk. Now she wasn't in an office with other people. Since Franc had left, she'd been using his office at times. She leaned her elbows on the desk and lifted her hand to the side of her neck, closing her eyes as she slowly massaged the area. Her heartbeat drummed in her ears.

You should have told him. You should have told him.

He'll never want this. He'll hate you.

The drum seemed to magnify—almost as if it were mocking her.

She tried to take long, steadying breaths. How long had it been since her last attack? There was no way this could be pregnancy-related. It was far too soon.

Pregnancy hormones couldn't affect her this quickly, could they?

Her brain was churning around a thousand thoughts. She needed to find out more. She needed to find out what happened next. What tests would she need? Could she do them in secret?

Her stomach flip-flopped over in protest.

The echo in her ears was finally quietening down, the pulse under her fingertips slowing. She leaned forward and put her head on the desk for a few seconds.

Part of her wanted to put her hand on her stomach—and part of her couldn't bear to. Her biggest dream and worst nightmare all rolled into one.

A baby she might probably not live to see.

A trickle of cold sweat slid down her back.

She was in a clinic. They did pregnancy tests in here all the time.

She could find one, and check right now. These days pregnancy tests could be positive from the first day of a missed period. She was nearly a week late.

She stood up quickly, grabbed her white coat and walked along the corridor towards one of the clinics. A few staff passed and nodded at her. It was like having a giant sign on her back.

Look at me, pregnant when I shouldn't be.

Her stomach twisted as she remembered how hard Gene had taken it when he'd had to break the news to Lea Keller about her pregnancy. It must have brought back memories and, from what he'd relayed, a hint of underlying sadness and mixed emotions. Did she really want to be the person who did that to him?

By the time she reached the white treatment room in the clinic her heart was thudding again. Only the drug cabinets were locked so she opened the supply cabinet and pulled out a pile of pregnancy tests, stuffing them in the pocket of her white coat.

It was pathetic. It almost felt as if alarms were going off around the place to let the world know exactly what she was doing.

One of the nurses came in at her back and she jumped. 'Hi, Cordelia,' the nurse said casually as she picked up an electronic blood-pressure monitor and walked back out.

Cordelia pressed her hands to her face. Yip. Her cheeks felt on fire.

She turned on her heel and walked smartly back down the corridor. The office had a private bathroom. She could do this in a matter of minutes.

But even though she felt ready, it had never been so difficult to pee on demand.

She sighed as she realised they often asked patients to do this, and plied them with water until they could manage.

Finally, she squeezed a few drops onto the stick and tried to breathe.

Two minutes had never seemed so long.

She washed her hands then, as the bathroom

was large, slid down the wall at the other side, keeping her eyes on her watch.

A picture of Rory laughing the night before danced into her head. A bolt of pain caught her. She'd just started being part of the little guy's life. He and Gene were the perfect partnership. How on earth would Rory understand? She wasn't clear how much he remembered Mindy—but he had mentioned the fact he thought she was in space in the stars above.

What if Gene had to tell him the same thing had happened to Cordelia? How much heartache could one kid take?

She leaned her head back against the cool, white tiles. What would she tell Franc? He had enough to deal with. He didn't need this too. The thought that she'd let him down made her feel sick to her stomach. The man who'd always had her back had known and understood about her illness. What would he think of her now?

Physicians shouldn't get 'accidentally' pregnant—particularly when they had a condition that could cost them their life. It was beyond stupid.

Maybe this pregnancy wouldn't be as taxing on her body as her cardiologist had always warned about. Maybe she could reach the end of a pregnancy and get the unbridled joy of holding her baby—their baby—in her arms? Couldn't she at least hope for that—no matter how unlikely it seemed?

The tap at the sink was dripping. It was almost like a countdown clock.

She glanced at her watch again. Her two minutes were up.

She closed her eyes, stood up and turned over the test.

Breathe. Breathe.

She opened her eyes.

Negative.

She blinked, then blinked again.

Negative. Negative.

She wasn't pregnant at all. Her period was just late.

Nausea hit her like a tidal wave and she leaned over the sink and retched, grabbing her hair with one hand. Her legs quivered beneath her. She wasn't pregnant. She wasn't going to die. Her baby wasn't going to die. Gene and Rory weren't going to have face losing a child and sibling, along with its mother.

She gripped the edge of the sink tightly, her knuckles turning white.

Relief. That's what she should be feeling right now. Pure and utter relief.

She could breathe again. She could forget about this.

But what if the pregnancy test was wrong? What if she was actually pregnant?

She stared at the word again. It was quite clear. Negative.

Her insides churned. So why wasn't she quite as overjoyed as she should be?

She leaned against the tiled wall again and let her legs slide her back down the wall to the floor.

She pulled her knees up to her chest and wrapped her arms around them, leaning her head on her knees.

For just a few minutes she'd actually *wanted* a baby. She had. She knew pregnancy would likely kill her. She knew her baby would be at risk. She knew the heartache it would cause both Gene and Rory but, still, a tiny selfish part of her had wanted it. She had. To hang with the risks.

What kind of a selfish monster was she?

Angry tears spilled down her cheeks.

'I thought I was past all this,' she murmured. 'I was.' She shook her head.

'Children aren't on the plan for me.' She said the words out loud, vainly hoping she could convince herself.

She leaned her head back against the hard tiles.

She might have convinced herself she was past it. But she'd never had a pregnancy scare before. She'd never been in a place where she thought she was actually falling for someone. She'd never had someone actually come out and ask her about her plans for the future.

And that's what she had now. The chance of a future with a gorgeous man and his son.

But she hadn't been honest with him. No, she hadn't been honest with *them*.

Because if she was going to tell Gene she was sick, she had to tell Rory too. She had to think about teaching a kid to dial the emergency number if she didn't wake up. She had to think about how her condition might progress and deteriorate in the future.

She could potentially become a mother figure to Rory. Would he eventually have two graves to visit?

It was horrid. It was decidedly morbid. But somewhere in amongst what seemed like fanciful thinking she needed a reality check.

There was a noise outside. Footsteps. 'Cordelia? Are you around?'

Gene. Her bag was lying on the floor next to the desk. He would know she was close. She quickly turned the tap on at the sink, hoping the sound of running water would give her a few more minutes' thinking time.

She splashed some water on her face, pulled her hair back into a ponytail, rinsed out her mouth and washed her hands.

There was no point even checking what she looked like in the mirror. She was pretty sure she already knew.

She stared at the test, sitting on the sink edge, the word 'Negative' still clear.

She picked it up and sighed.

The most difficult conversation in the world had to start somewhere.

She'd left this too long already.

CHAPTER TEN

WHERE WAS SHE? Her bag was there, as well as her heels, which were lying sideways on the floor.

There was the sound of running water, followed by a few sniffs. He stood off to one side. He had to talk to her. He had to let her know what the research was starting to show. Things were looking good.

There had been significant progress in one of the trials. Even though the data still had to be thoroughly analysed he had a really good feeling about it. It gave him hope. A large percentage of the patients on this trial were showing signs of improvement. Their cardiac function had improved, their blood results were stable and they had few—if any—side effects. This could be a turning point in the progression of cardiomyopathy. And he wanted to share it with the person who shared his enthusiasm and passion most—the woman he wanted to share everything with.

'Cordelia?' he called again, a little more cautiously. Was she all right in there?

The bathroom door opened. The bright light shone behind her, highlighting her pale skin and the dark circles under her eyes. She looked… drained.

He stepped forward immediately, putting one hand at her elbow. 'What's wrong? Aren't you feeling well?'

She didn't speak, even though her mouth opened. It was her eyes. The expression in her eyes. As if something terrible had just happened.

'Cordelia?' he said yet again, this time more concerned. Maybe something had happened to Professor Helier.

Then he looked down. He'd been a doctor for a long time. He recognised a pregnancy test at twenty paces. It was dangling from her fingertips.

He stepped back as his mind leapt to a thousand possibilities and his brain tried to control his words.

It took less than a second for his heart to start racing in his chest. Thrill. Wonder. Excitement. Then just as quickly he realised that the expression on her face didn't match the thoughts in his head.

'Cordelia, are you pregnant?'

She shook her head as a tear trailed down her cheek. He lifted his finger instantly to brush it away. She held up the test so he could glance at the word. *Negative.*

It was like something inside him sagged. He pulled her into a hug. She still hadn't spoken but he could feel her body tremble.

'It's okay. Did you think you were pregnant? Don't be upset. I know we didn't plan anything. I know it's soon. But it wouldn't be the end of the world, would it? That's the kind of thing I wanted to talk to you about. I guess we should have that chat now.'

He kept holding her, feeling the shaky rise and fall of her chest against his. She hadn't hugged him back; her hands still hung limply by her sides.

He reached up and stroked her hair, pulling her head back a little so he could see her face.

He kissed her forehead then her nose. 'Talk to me, honey.'

Something didn't feel quite right. He could understand she might have been a little shocked at thinking she was pregnant. But right now he couldn't quite figure if she was devastated at *not* being pregnant or devastated at *thinking* she might be pregnant.

Right now his brain was focusing on that initial feeling of elation. Another baby. A brother or sister for Rory?

He'd always thought he might like to have more children under a different set of circumstances. But up until a few seconds ago he hadn't realised just how much.

He was disappointed Cordelia wasn't pregnant. *Disappointed.*

And that made him catch his breath at all the implications that went along with that.

A new relationship. Potentially a new home. A new life. A life with a partner for him, a new mom for Rory and maybe—in the future—a new baby.

Cordelia stiffened in his arms. She stepped back, holding up her hands in front of her. She shook her head and he watched her trying to catch her breath.

'This…this…' She was still holding the pregnancy test. 'It can't happen, it can't…can't… happen.' She shook her head more fiercely. *'Ever.'*

Every tiny little hair on his body stood on end at the way she spat out that final word. He stepped back too.

'You don't want kids?' Was that what she was telling him?

She flung up her hands and let out an exasperated whimper. Her jaw clenched and her voice shook. 'It's not that I don't want kids. It's that I *can't* have kids. Not if I want to keep living. '

Now he was completely confused. She'd thought she was pregnant. So she must be able to have kids. She must be able to get pregnant. If she couldn't, why did she need a pregnancy test?

'You're not making any sense.' His brain couldn't quite compute.

She threw the test in the trash can next to his feet. 'Why do you think I work here? Why do you think I work at the institute?'

She was angry. She was angry at him and he couldn't understand why.

'I don't know. You said you wanted to, you loved it.' Why did he feel as if he was the only person in the room who didn't have a clue what was going on?

She leaned forward and poked him in the chest. 'You work here because of Rory. You do cardiac research because, ultimately, you want to find a cure for your son.'

He nodded warily. 'Yes, and I've been up front about that from the start.'

She let out a wry laugh. She shook her head and pressed her hand to her chest. 'I work here because of Wolff-Parkinson-White syndrome. I work here because my condition meant that I could no longer work on the wards. My symptoms got so bad, I couldn't be in a clinical area full time. You think I wanted to leave clinical work? You think I spent all those years training as a doctor not to actually *be* one?'

It was like a chill over his skin. A cool, prickling breeze.

Pieces of the jigsaw puzzle started to slot into

place in his brain. The way she'd evaded a few questions. The day she'd been sick.

He opened his mouth. But the words were stuck. She'd known. She'd known about her condition for how long? And she hadn't mentioned it to him. Not at work, not at home and not in bed.

His brain was still trying to process this as he spoke out loud. 'Why didn't you tell me?'

She laughed. She actually laughed.

She threw up her hands again and started pacing around the office. 'How do I tell you that? What part of the conversation starts with "Wait till I tell you about my medical condition"?'

His answer was sharp. He could feel anger rise in his chest. Another woman with a cardiac condition who hadn't told him. A different cardiac condition but one that had risks. Risks he hadn't been told about. 'That's not fair and you know it. You've had more than one opportunity you could have told me about this.'

He frowned. 'Women with Wolff-Parkinson-White have babies. Some people don't even know they have the condition when they get pregnant.' He was just saying what he knew out loud.

'Not me. My cardiologist warned me years ago about the severity of my condition and what pregnancy could do. He knows me. He didn't sugar-coat it.'

He opened his mouth to respond but she stopped pacing for a second, hands on her hips. Her hair had become unravelled from its normally groomed style and was mussed around her face. She gave him a sideways glance.

That little flare of anger ignited again. It was almost as if she wasn't giving him permission to speak.

Her voice was low and laced with anger. 'How could I tell you, Gene? You'd just told me about Rory and his mother. How could I tell you that I've got a condition that means I should never get pregnant? You've been down that road. It's not one you'll want to walk again.' She closed her eyes and he could see the tremble along her jawline. It was almost like she was speaking the words that were currently racing around in his brain. Her words came out with force.

'I didn't know anything would happen between us. You were only supposed to be here a month.' She opened her eyes and gestured with one hand. 'I didn't even know about Rory.'

'And when you did?' Gene stepped right up close to her. His anger was starting to make sense in his head now. He was a parent. He was Rory's only parent. Rory was his first and foremost priority.

Maybe the magic of the Geneva setting had messed with his mind? Something certainly had.

This time her voice wasn't quite so strong. She breathed in, in awkward jerks. 'I probably should have kept my distance. I struggle around young kids.' She looked over at the trash can. 'I thought I'd come to terms with things a long time ago.'

He couldn't describe the feeling swamping over him. Disappointment. Disillusionment. It was like watching a bright balloon he'd been holding slip from his hands and float out over the nearby mountains.

He couldn't quite work out how he felt about all this. 'You have a condition that could kill you if you get pregnant. And you didn't tell me.

You were sleeping with me—but you didn't tell me. You're a doctor. You knew the risks. And you didn't think to share them?'

She turned on him. 'Don't say it like that. You think I wasn't careful? Of course I was. I've always taken care of contraception. I've never wanted to be in a position like this.'

'So what happened?' He couldn't help the strangulated sound that came out as he walked away and ran his fingers through his hair. 'We'd been talking about having a future together. We'd been talking about possibilities. If I'd known about this—'

'You'd what?' she snapped. The words came out like a challenge.

'I'd have worn a condom!' he shouted back. 'When there's a high risk, two types of contraception are better than one.' It was just as much his responsibility as it was hers. Inside he was cringing. Yes, he'd asked her. Yes, she'd reassured him.

But shouldn't he have taken matters into his own hands anyway—even without any risks?

'What if the test wasn't negative, Cordelia?' His stomach was churning now. It had leapt at the thought of another child. He'd actually had a few seconds of pure joy at the thought of bringing another child into the world with a woman he actually loved.

'What if we were standing here right now, and you were telling me you'd just given yourself a death sentence?' His voice almost cracked. 'And I'd caused it?'

Her head dipped but her voice was clear. 'That's why I'm telling you now, Gene.' She walked over to the glass wall and put her hands on the glass, staring out at the backdrop that was normally behind them. Her head bent forward, resting against the glass.

'This can't happen again,' she said, her words almost a whisper.

'You're right. It can't.'

It came out before he could think straight. What she'd just thrown at him was enormous. He'd never really considered a partner before in terms of health.

The Mindy thing had sideswiped him completely. He knew what being completely unprepared felt like.

He never wanted to feel like that again. And he certainly didn't want to expose his son to that.

Her green gaze met his. It was almost as if she'd built a shield over her eyes. They were glassy and detached-looking.

He straightened himself up. 'You should have told me about your health condition. I'm assuming that Professor Helier knew?'

She gave the briefest of nods.

'Then in his absence you had a responsibility to tell me too. We are living under the same roof, working in the same clinic. Treating patients clinically.' He closed his eyes—just for a second. 'That day in the cath lab. You had an attack, didn't you?' He didn't even wait for a response. 'You should have been honest.'

'I was. I told you I had to step outside.' There was an air of desperation in her voice.

He moved closer to her. 'Not. Good. Enough. If the doctor I'm working with has a condition that can affect her patient care at any point then I need to know about it. I need to know to look for the signs and intervene if need be.'

She flinched and he could tell she hated those

words. Hated the fact they were right. Hated the fact he'd said them out loud.

'Don't tell me what I can and can't do.'

He turned to walk away. 'I'm not. I'm taking responsibility for your condition. Something that you clearly haven't. I have no interest in being your cardiologist. But I do have an interest in the welfare of the patients in this clinic. Don't do any procedures without another physician present.'

'I never have.'

'And if you don't tell your colleagues, I will.' He headed for the door. 'This isn't over, Cordelia.'

He felt betrayed, both personally, and professionally.

The future he'd dared to imagine in his head for the first time in four years had just disappeared in a puff of smoke.

And he had no idea what to tell his son.

CHAPTER ELEVEN

BY THE TIME she'd picked herself up at least an hour had passed.

The little white stick in the trash can had unearthed a whole host of feelings she hadn't been ready for, or prepared for.

A few days ago she'd dared to hope the life she'd always dreamed of might actually come true. A life with Gene and with Rory.

And that had been enough. That had been more than enough. More than she'd ever hoped for. A gorgeous man who loved her as much as she loved him, and a beautiful child she could love just as much.

A few days of hope. A few days of bliss.

And now it had all come crashing down around her.

All because of a moment of madness. A tiny possibility that had made her realise how much she'd been hiding from herself.

That a child of her own *really* was never possible.

But she hadn't shared that with Gene. She hadn't let him decide to love her despite the fact there would never be any more kids.

Something deep down inside told her that could have been a possibility.

And instead of taking the time and chance to sit down with him and let him know, she'd gone in completely the wrong direction.

Of course she wasn't pregnant. But because the seed had been planted in her head, she'd realised how much she wanted it.

It was like stepping back ten years—when her cardiologist had first spoken to her about the severity of her disease and its implications.

She pressed her head against the glass. It didn't matter how picturesque the setting. How fabulous her workplace.

Everything was falling apart around her.

She pressed her hand to her chest. How ironic that the one time she felt so exhausted and stressed was the one time her WPW didn't kick in.

She sucked in a breath. It almost felt like

someone was sitting on her shoulders, weighing her down to the floor.

Gene had looked so angry. She'd seen that first little flicker, that hint of a smile and flash of delight in his eyes at the thought of a pregnancy.

It had sparked off every wrong emotion in her. Every spark of anger, regret and disillusionment. There had never been a moment in her life where she'd felt quite so inadequate. That tiny smile and glimmer of excitement had let her know that she could never give Gene those things. She could never build a family with him, share a pregnancy. And the emotions had just all tumbled from there.

Now he was angry. He felt deceived and betrayed by her.

She didn't blame him.

The person she was most disappointed in was herself.

She sucked in another deep breath and glanced at her watch.

How could she go back to the house? There was no way she could live under the same roof.

She couldn't bear it, and she was sure neither could he.

If she left now, she could make it back to the house and empty her things—take them back to her apartment in Geneva.

She'd overstayed her welcome in Professor Helier's home.

It was time to move out.

He didn't see her for the rest of the day.

He didn't want to see her.

His head was still full of a million questions that just seemed to churn around in his mind.

By the time he picked up Rory at nursery his head was starting to throb.

'Can we play hide and seek, Daddy?' Rory asked.

'Maybe later. We need to get home and fix dinner. Then it will probably be time for bed.'

Rory frowned. 'But I want to play hide and seek. I've found a new hiding place at home. I want to hide there.'

Gene sighed. 'Not now, Rory,' he snapped, then instantly regretted it as Rory winced.

He'd managed to avoid Cordelia at the institute but it would be much harder to avoid her at home. Maybe he should take Rory out for dinner to help prevent any awkward scenes back at the house? Maybe he should look for an alternative apartment to rent? Anything would be better than avoiding each other at home. How on earth would he explain that to Rory?

But two minutes after they reached the house with takeout food he knew something was wrong.

Rory rushed up the stairs then came running back down. 'Something's wrong with Delia's room.'

'What do you mean?' When her car hadn't been outside he'd just assumed Cordelia was working late.

Rory wrinkled his nose. 'Nothing's there.'

Gene turned from where he'd been about to cut the pizza, closed the takeaway box again and climbed the stairs in long strides.

Somehow he knew what he was about to find. And his stomach clenched in the most horrible way.

Cordelia had left in a hurry. The dresser drawers were still slightly open. The wardrobe doors not closed properly. The bathroom had been emptied and wiped down and the bed stripped.

Rory was still frowning. He turned to face Gene and shook his head. 'Where's Delia, Daddy?' He picked up the pillow on the bed. 'Her teddy-bear jammies are gone.'

Gene sat down on the edge of the bed. 'I guess she must have decided to move out,' he said hoarsely. 'This isn't her real house. She has another place she can stay.'

It took Rory a few seconds to speak. 'But why wouldn't she want to stay with us? And why wouldn't she tell us she was going someplace else?' Gene's heart squeezed in his chest. Rory's voice sounded shaky and his eyes looked a little glazed.

Gene reached over and pulled Rory up onto his knee. He chose his words carefully. 'Sometimes adults have a difference of opinion.'

'What?'

Gene tried again. 'They sometimes fight.'

'Did you fight with Delia?'

Gene sighed. 'Maybe.'

'Then just say sorry, Daddy. She'll know you

mean it. And she'll come back. She'll play hide and seek with me. We can all play together.'

Gene pressed his lips together and tried to find the right words.

Pieces in his head started to slot together.

He'd been so angry earlier. So indignant about things. Thinking about himself and about Rory—about how Cordelia's condition could impact on them all.

He hadn't thought about *her*. Hadn't thought about how devastated she'd looked when she'd gripped the pregnancy test in her hand.

He hadn't thought about what *this* might feel like. This...emptiness. This feeling of complete loss.

He loved her. He completely and utterly loved her.

It had kind of sneaked up on him. Taken him unawares.

And now that he realised just how much she meant to him, it completely terrified him.

It was official. He was heartbroken.

How could he possibly be? He hadn't even told Cordelia that he loved her yet. He hadn't even realised that he loved her yet.

But the emptiness of the creaky house—the way that every noise they made seemed to echo down the corridor and bounce off the walls— just seemed to magnify the feelings in his heart.

Of course he loved Rory. That was always going to be a given.

But the last few weeks, spending time with Cordelia, had really opened his eyes. Neither of them were permanent residents in this house, but being here with her had made this place feel like a home instead of a house.

Now he understood her initial reluctance around Rory. She had been trying to protect herself. But watching how their relationship had blossomed and grown had been…special. It was clear she'd liked spending time with Rory, and Rory, in turn, had loved being around her. He couldn't deny it. Having a woman in his life was clearly good for Rory. Gene had always been clear in his head that he could be mom and dad to his little boy. But it was clear that Rory found different qualities in Cordelia than he found in his dad.

Part of Gene hated that. Especially now.

Had that affected how he felt about Cordelia?

Sure. He and Rory were a partnership. He could never be with someone who couldn't love his child. But Cordelia? She was already part way there—if not the whole way.

He ran his fingers through Rory's hair. The little head was resting on his shoulder. 'I don't think Cordelia wants to play hide and seek right now, honey.'

Rory lifted his head and narrowed his gaze. 'You don't want to say sorry, do you?'

Every muscle in Gene's body tensed. Children could be so astute sometimes. 'I don't know,' he said.

Rory's face fell. He looked as if he could cry. 'But I asked if I could pick. I pick Delia. I told you that, Daddy.'

Gene wrapped his arms around his son's body. There was so much more to this than he could explain.

'I thought I'd picked Delia too, honey. But I'm not sure that Delia wants to be picked. I'm not sure that she's ready to pick us back.'

As he said the words out loud he realised how true they were.

Yes, he was angry.

Yes, he was hurt she hadn't told him the truth.

Yes, he'd had a glimmer of hope at the thought of her being pregnant.

But with hope came despair.

If she'd been truthful and given him the chance to choose, he would have chosen her over having any more family.

Yes, he would choose someone with a chronic condition—one that someday could kill them.

He knew the risks. He knew ultimately she could go into heart failure or need a transplant.

But these were all ifs.

Next year he could have cancer. Next year he could have a stroke.

He might think he wasn't at risk—but what did anyone really know?

So much was going through his mind.

And he didn't have a clue what to do next.

CHAPTER TWELVE

FOR THE FIRST time in her life, Cordelia Greenway didn't want to go to work.

Every minute at work meant trying to avoid Gene. It was awkward. Impersonal. And totally against what she wanted to do.

There was so much she should sit down and talk to him about. She wasn't stupid. She knew she owed him an apology.

But that could result in something that would ultimately make her feel a million times worse than she currently did.

That could result in him telling her that he didn't want to see her, he didn't want to spend time with her, and he certainly wouldn't be building any kind of life with her.

Why should he pick someone who was broken when he could easily find someone who was whole? Someone without any disease in their heart, someone who could help him fulfil his dream of expanding his family.

Finding out she couldn't be with the man and child she loved and adored would feel like the final nail in the coffin.

She'd always felt as if she fell a little short. It was odd that parts of her body she had no control over could do that to a person.

There was a world of psychological research that told her these feelings had been studied the world over. She wasn't the only human being who felt like this.

But the research didn't matter to her.

The only thing that mattered to her was the here and now.

Her condition could remain the same for the next ten years. Or this time next year she could end up on the heart-transplant list.

Did she want Rory to see her sick?

Something washed over like a black storm cloud.

Did she want to see Rory sick?

Because that was just as likely to happen.

Her reaction was instantaneous. She wrapped

her arms around herself and started rocking. It was her worst nightmare.

Of course she would want to be there. Of course she would want to by Gene's side so they could hold Rory's hand and stroke his forehead.

No matter how much she hated herself right now, she couldn't picture her life without these people.

She loved them.

She loved them with every part of her being. Every breath that she took. Every fibre in her body, and every beat of her imperfect heart.

Her hands shook as she sucked in a breath.

She reached for her jacket and car keys.

It didn't matter that she didn't want to go to work. It didn't matter that she was scared.

It didn't matter that this could all blow up in her face.

All that mattered was that she try.

CHAPTER THIRTEEN

HE PICKED UP the phone as soon as it rang—half hoping it might be Cordelia.

'Dr Du Bois—Gene, how are you?'

It took a few seconds to recognise the husky voice.

'Professor Helier? Is everything okay?'

The old man cleared his throat. 'How are things at the institute? How is the research project? I was very interested in what you sent me.'

Gene pressed his lips together. In his excitement the other day he'd forwarded the preliminary research findings on to Professor Helier. He knew the timing might be wrong, but this work was Professor Helier's life—and he'd asked to be kept up to date on all progress.

Gene nodded. It was really the only piece of good news that he had.

'I'm so glad you've had a chance to look at it. The provisional findings are promising. This

could be the start of something really significant.'

'It could. It really could. In fact, that's why
I'm calling you.'

'It is?' He was curious, but his insides were
churning. He would have to be honest with Professor Helier. He would have to let him know
how things were between himself and Cordelia. This research was so important. He didn't
want to compromise it in any way.

'It is.' Professor Helier cleared his throat. 'I
have something else I have to ask you.'

The hairs prickled at the back of his neck.
Gene kept his voice steady. 'What is it?'

Professor Helier sounded hesitant. 'My sister
is obviously very unwell. And knowing I don't
have much time left with her has made me re-
evaluate a few things. I'm old, Gene. And I
don't have as many years left as I might wish
for. I need to plan for someone to take over from
me at the institute.'

'But that will be Cordelia surely? She's your
second in command.'

'Yes, you're right. It will be Cordelia. She's
my natural choice. But...'

His voice tailed off for a second as he seemed to choose his words carefully. 'I think it would be best if she had someone she could share the workload with. Someone who is equally passionate about the work we do here as she is.'

Gene closed his eyes for a few seconds. It was clear Professor Helier knew about Cordelia's condition but wasn't going to betray her trust. He respected her that much—just like Gene should.

'I'd like you to be that person, Gene. The truth is, I've watched the work that you'd done over the past few years and was delighted to get the chance to invite you here. I'm sorry we've not had the chance to work together, but circumstances—'

'Of course. I understand,' said Gene quickly.

'I'd like you to consider what I'm offering you. Everyone at the institute is very impressed by your work.'

'Not everyone,' he said quietly.

'What?' asked Professor Helier.

Gene breathed in, 'Have you spoken to Cordelia yet?'

'No. But I'm sure she'll be delighted. Over the last few weeks she's been very complimentary about your work.'

Gene ran his fingers through his hair. Somehow he didn't think so.

'There's a lot to think about.'

'I know that. That's why I called you first. To give you some time to consider my offer. I'll still remain as Head of the Institute. But I'd like you and Cordelia to lead the two research teams, to work together.'

Gene let out a sigh. 'Professor Helier, things might be a little more difficult than you think.'

'Why? Don't you like the institute? Or is it Geneva?'

Gene breathed deeply. 'I love the institute. And I love Geneva. But…' he knew he had to say the words out loud '…there's someone else that I love more. And the last thing I want to do is make her feel uncomfortable.'

There was silence at the end of the phone. It was the longest pause, and he could almost hear Professor Helier's brain ticking.

'This her? Is this…a mutual acquaintance of ours?'

Gene cringed. Most of the staff at the institute knew that something had been going on between him and Cordelia. It was likely that Professor Helier would eventually hear too.

'It could be,' he said hesitantly.

'Dr Du Bois, it doesn't matter how wonderful a researcher you are. It doesn't matter what the possibilities for the future work could be. You need to know that my loyalties will always lie with Cordelia. She's worked tirelessly for me over the last few years. She's the most dedicated doctor I've ever worked with. She's family to me.'

Gene felt like some teenager being told off. But he had to admire the loyalty that Professor Helier had for Cordelia.

Professor Helier continued. 'Maybe I was wrong to offer you this position.'

'Maybe you were,' Gene finished for him.

'Let's take the job and the institute out of the equation—even though I was flattered by your offer. I can't do anything to make Cordelia unhappy, and me working here might make things difficult. Let me talk to her. We need a chance to work things out together. I need a chance to convince her that I, and Rory, want to be part of her life.'

'In that case, I will leave things with you. Good luck, Dr Du Bois.'

Gene hung up the phone. Rory was in nursery. He'd checked on all the patients this morning—there was no one he currently had concerns about, except Cordelia.

It was time to be true to his heart.

He could lose Cordelia. He could lose her now. He could lose her in a few years because of her condition or he could spend the next thirty years with her.

No one on this planet knew how long they had.

Not him. Not Cordelia. And not Rory.

Was it wrong to put Rory in a position where he could love Cordelia then lose her? He'd asked himself this question so many times in the last few hours.

He shook his head. It was time to stop asking what if.

It was time to stop second-guessing.

It was time to follow the lead from the most important organ of the body.

His heart.

CHAPTER FOURTEEN

SHE SCANNED THE NURSERY. There was no familiar mop of blond hair. Panic hovered just above her chest. She'd been through the whole institute and there was no sign of Gene. No one could tell her where he was. A few people had seen him earlier but were not quite sure where he'd gone next. Would he actually leave without telling her?

Then a brainwave had hit her. If Rory was here, Gene must be close by. The nursery. The place she should probably have tried first.

She gestured one of the nursery staff over. 'Is Rory Du Bois in today? I can't see him.'

Emma rolled her eyes. 'He's in a bit of a mood today.' She pointed to the corner of the nursery floor. 'He's been in the playhouse for the last hour, refusing to talk to anyone. We've all been in there and tried to persuade him to come out.

But Rory is one determined little guy.' She gave Cordelia a sympathetic smile. 'Be my guest.'

Cordelia breathed a sigh of relief and hurried across the floor to the brightly coloured plastic playhouse. She paused at the red door and gave it a knock. 'Rory? Rory, are you in there? It's Cordelia. Will you come out and see me?'

'No,' came the firm little voice, then, after a pause, 'But you can come in.'

Cordelia looked down and hitched up her skirt with her hands. Thankfully, she hadn't changed out of her baseball boots this morning, so she pushed the door open with one hand and crawled inside.

Rory was sitting in one of the corners. All the blue shutters on the windows were closed, his arms were folded across his chest and a frown was on his face.

'Hey, little guy. What's up?'

He stuck out his bottom lip.

She tried to pull herself completely inside the cramped playhouse. 'This isn't like you,' she said as she adjusted her position, pulling her legs up to her chest. 'You always play with the other kids.'

'I'm not talking to anyone,' he said crossly.

Cordelia tried not to smile. She'd felt a bit like that herself yesterday.

'Okay.' She nodded. 'Why not?'

He glared at her. 'I picked you.'

Her breath caught in her throat. 'What?'

Rory's brow was so furrowed she could barely see his eyes. 'I picked you. And Daddy picked you. But he said you didn't want to be picked.'

Cordelia shook her head. 'What do you mean—you picked me?'

Rory held up his hands as if it was the most obvious thing in the world. 'I picked you to be my new mommy.'

Cordelia choked. 'What?' Her brain started to spin and tears pricked the corners of her eyes.

Rory looked at her again. 'I picked you to be my new mommy. And Daddy said he'd picked you too.' He scowled at her. 'But you didn't want to be picked.'

Cordelia put her hand up to her chest. 'Who said that, Rory? Who said I didn't want to be picked?'

Rory looked puzzled now. 'Daddy. He said he

didn't think you wanted us to pick you. Why don't you want us, Cordelia?'

A tear slid down her cheek as she shook her head fiercely. She wrapped her arms around Rory and pulled him close. 'Oh, I want you, honey. You've no idea how much I want you both. Us grown-ups are complicated. We get mad at each other. We do stupid things. And we say even sillier things. Don't think for a second that I don't want you, honey. Of course I do. You and your dad are the best people I've ever met. I would pick you a million times over.'

There was a noise at the door and a red-faced Gene appeared. He looked into the cramped playhouse. It was pretty clear he must have heard what she'd just said.

She swallowed, her mouth instantly dry as their gazes met.

She'd come here ready to fight for them both. She regretted what she'd said. She so regretted not being truthful. But would she get a chance to say any of that?

'Room for one more?' Gene asked. 'I heard there was a party going on in here.'

Cordelia bit her lip. 'I think we can squish up

a bit.' She shifted over next to Rory as Gene's long jeans-clad limbs tried to clamber into the plastic playhouse.

By the time he got inside, Gene's knees were practically up to his chin. His arms were against Cordelia's and their heads close together.

Once he was settled he gave her a sideways glance. 'I was looking for you.'

'You were?'

He nodded. Her heart started that crazy irregular beating again. But this wasn't a WPW attack. This was just pure and utter hope.

'I was looking for you too.'

His head tilted to the side and he gave her a curious stare.

'I wanted to apologise,' she said quickly as she looked at Rory. For a second she tried to think of a particular way to say things. A way that Rory might not understand. But she quickly realised that was wrong. She wanted both of these people in her life and it was time to be honest with them both.

'I wanted to say sorry that I didn't tell you about my condition. I should have trusted you. I should have told you.'

'What's your condition?' asked Rory innocently.

She nodded her head slowly and turned to the little boy. She pointed to his chest. 'You know how things can be wrong with people's hearts?'

'That's what Daddy does.'

She nodded again. 'I know. Well... I have something wrong with my heart too. Sometimes it goes too quickly and I have to try and slow it down. It can make me a little sick sometimes and I have to be careful.'

Rory wrinkled his nose. 'Is it dangerous?'

The million-dollar question. Gene's dark eyes were fixed firmly on hers. Would he want her to stop at this point? Maybe she had no right to tell Rory the truth.

But the look in Gene's eyes made her skin tingle. There was nothing but pure and utter support in his gaze.

She gave the slightest nod. 'It can be. Or it could be in the future.' She reached over and squeezed Rory's hand. 'None of us know how we will be in the future. I could get sick, or I could be fine. I just can't say for sure.' She swallowed and tapped her chest again with her other hand. 'There are some things that I do know, though.'

'Like what?' You couldn't beat a child's curiosity for cutting to the chase.

She kept her voice steady. 'Like, for me, it wouldn't be a good idea to have a baby.'

'A baby? Why would you want to have a baby?' Rory looked over at Gene. 'I don't want a brother or sister. I've seen some of the diapers in the nursery.' He scrunched up his face. 'Yeuch!'

Cordelia laughed as her heart swelled in her chest. 'I guess I don't need to worry, then.' She lifted her eyes warily to Gene, trying not to let her voice shake. 'Unless, of course, your daddy wants to have more babies.'

'Oh, no,' said Rory quickly as he waved his hand between him and Gene. 'We're a team. It's just us. There's no room for babies.'

Cordelia bit her bottom lip. 'No room for anyone?'

'Oh, there's room for you. I told you. I told Daddy. I picked you. You can be in our team.'

She blinked back the tears and looked at Gene

as Rory slid his little hand into hers. 'What do you think?'

She was holding her breath. Everything depended on what came next. Was it really possible to hope this much?

Gene put his hand on Rory's soft hair. 'Oh, we talked. We talked about how much we loved having you around. We talked about how much we wanted to see you every day.' His voice changed a little. 'We talked about how empty the house seemed without you there. We missed you.'

His gaze didn't waver from hers. 'We don't need any more kids. We're happy just as we are. I have a feeling that Rory might keep us busy for the next thirty years.' He raised his eyebrows. 'If you're up for the job, that is.'

She was still holding her breath. She'd heard a little word in amongst all that. Was she brave enough to use it? She looked at the tiny weathered lines around Gene's eyes. The expression of love on his face. Even now, his gaze flickered between her and Rory. His work shirt was completely crumpled, halfway tucked into his jeans. His brown cowboy boots were only half in the playhouse, because those longs legs were struggling with the cramped space.

She took a deep breath. Now she couldn't stop her voice shaking as she let out a nervous laugh. 'I am *so* up for this job. I love you guys. I really do. I never expected to meet people like you two, and feel like this.' She nodded her head and looked down at Rory. 'You don't know how special it makes me feel to know that you've picked me. But you need to know, I picked you too. I absolutely want to see you every day.' She took another breath. She was willing to do just about anything to make this work. 'If that means I need to move someplace else to be near you guys, then I'll do that.'

Gene cleared his throat. 'Franc called.'

'He did?'

Gene nodded. 'I might have let him know that something was going on. He asked me to stay.' He paused for a second. 'For good.'

'He did?' She repeated it again.

He gave her a smile that sent a million little sparks flying across her skin. 'I told him I couldn't say yes until I'd spoken to you. I didn't know what you might say. I didn't want to compromise your working environment if you didn't want us around.'

She shook her head fiercely, 'Why on earth wouldn't I want you around?' The tears started to flow freely. 'Of course I want you both around.' She slid her arm around Rory's shoulder and held her hand out towards Gene. 'I want you both around always.'

Rory blinked and gave a small smile. 'Did you bring the present we bought a few days ago?' he asked his dad.

Gene laughed. 'I did.' He looked around, and gave a smile as he shook his head. 'But we might need to get out of here first. I don't know if a plastic playhouse is where we really want to give this present.' He bent down and whispered in Rory's ear, 'We're supposed to be cool.'

Cordelia's stomach was still in knots. But this time, instead of dark twisty knots, the knots were more flutters of excitement. Gene crawled out of the playhouse first, followed by an excited Rory. She tried to tug her skirt back down as she crawled out behind them. Gene's hand came down and he pulled her up into his arms.

There was something so reassuring about

being back in his arms. 'You're really okay with not having any more kids?' she whispered.

'We already have the best kid on the planet.' He smiled. 'Why would we need any more?'

He reached over, his thumb brushing away the tear on her cheek. 'No more secrets, okay? You heard our kid, we're a team. We can do this.' He smiled again. 'Someone pretty important once told me we have a whole wide world out there. Let's go and live this life—together.'

She reached her hands up around his neck and smiled. 'I wonder who that might have been?'

He gave a nod, kissed her cheek, then stepped back. 'Give me a second.' He took a few long strides and picked up a plastic carrier bag sitting near the nursery entrance. He came back with a twinkle in his eye. 'I want you to know just how hard it was to find this in Geneva. And it had to be the right colour—Rory insisted.'

She stared at the large shape in the plastic bag, trying to decipher what it could be. Gene's voice was low. 'I know it's not an engagement ring. We'll get to that later. Or maybe we'll even skip it and just go for the wedding.'

'We will?' She smiled.

He put his hand in the bag. 'And we have something special for you to wear on our wedding day. Because we all have to match. I have mine. Rory has his. And now you...' he pulled something from the bag '...have yours.'

She laughed out loud as the large bright red Stetson—that matched her baseball boots—was put on her head. It nearly covered her eyes.

'You bought me a Stetson?'

He pulled her into his arms and dropped a kiss on her lips. 'Of course I bought you a Stetson. Haven't you heard? You're just about to marry a cowboy?'

And she wrapped her arms around his neck and kissed her cowboy, with the backdrop of the snow-topped mountains, surrounded by a gaggle of rowdy toddlers.

Things couldn't be more perfect.

* * * * *

LET'S TALK

For exclusive extracts, competitions
and special offers, find us online:

f facebook.com/millsandboon

◎ @millsandboonuk

𝕏 @millsandboon

Or get in touch on 0844 844 1351*

For all the latest titles coming soon,
visit millsandboon.co.uk/nextmonth

*Calls cost 7p per minute plus your phone company's price per
minute access charge

Want even more
ROMANCE?

Join our bookclub today!

'Mills & Boon books, the perfect way to escape for an hour or so.'

Miss W. Dyer

'Excellent service, promptly delivered and very good subscription choices.'

Miss A. Pearson

'You get fantastic special offers and the chance to get books before they hit the shops'

Mrs V. Hall

Visit millsandbook.co.uk/Bookclub and save on brand new books.

MILLS & BOON